ROCKY POINT DAWN
Rocky Point Series, Book Six

BARBARA MCMAHON

Chapter One

Callie carefully pressed the off button of her phone. She wished for the olden days when she could have slammed it down after first yelling at Jocelyn Warren to stop calling her every day in her attempts to micro-manage everything.

But discretion being the better part of business life, Callie'd kept her voice calm, sharing none of her escalating frustration with the woman on the other end.

Proud of her self-control, she waited until the connection had been cut before giving a discreet "Eeeek!"

"Lord, please grant me patience. I know she's having a hard time. But she's driving me crazy!"

Not for the first time since Randolph Artemis had died, Callie wished he was still around and running the art gallery in Rocky Point so she could escalate problems to him. But the buck stopped with her these days.

Inheriting the small art gallery turned out to be a mixed blessing. Normally she loved her calling, even when dealing with difficult artists like Jocelyn Warren. Actually if Callie and Jocelyn's conversation had centered around Jocelyn's work, it'd have been so much easier to deal with.

Instead they were involved in an ongoing battle to determine how many of Jocelyn's son's paintings would be displayed in a public retrospective Callie had agreed to host at the gallery.

They were in the final stages of planning, less than two weeks left before opening night. Callie wished Jocelyn would let her do what she did well and go back to her painting.

She leaned back in her chair, rubbing her temples. She was getting a headache as she often did after dealing with the temperamental artist.

Unfortunately, not all of it could be attributed to Jocelyn. Some of it was caused by pure guilt.

Keeping a life-changing secret wasn't easy.

At one time not too long ago, Callie expected Jocelyn to become her mother-in-law.

Now she wondered if they could have been so related and not end up killing each. It was growing harder and harder to deal with her since Tommy died.

Her own emotions were in turmoil. The hurt and grief had gradually eased. Sometimes she could go for a day or so without focusing on what happened.

Then Jocelyn would call and bring everything to the forefront again.

She hoped time would heal the relationship. Once the show was over, there'd be no necessity for daily check-ins by Jocelyn.

I know she's grieving, Lord, so please give me enough compassion to deal kindly with her.

"Callie, I need you out here right away!" her assistant,

Suzanne, called from the gallery.

Suzanne was usually a calm and even tempered young woman. She and Callie had worked together for almost a year and she was a highly valued employee. What caused that note of panic in her voice?

It had to be an emergency for her to yell from the public gallery.

Callie dashed across her small, cluttered office. Off-limits to all but closest friends or long time business associates, the office reflected none of the serenity and beauty of the displays in the gallery.

Stacks of papers cluttered the desk. A utilitarian file cabinet sat against one wall. The furnishings were functional and serviceable, nothing fancy.

Randolph had made the showroom a beautiful and inviting haven for the art he displayed.

He had no desire to make his office anything but utilitarian. And Callie had continued in his steps.

She opened the door and stepped into another world. Paintings graced the walls, discreetly illuminated by full spectrum, high tech lights. Thick neutral carpeting muffled footsteps. Scattered artfully on freestanding pedestals around the large space stood sculptures of renown.

She offered metal, stone and glass objets d'art, as well as the paintings for which the gallery was known. Randolph had built the business in the historic Maine town to cater to locals and tourists alike.

Callie was doing her best to carry on.

Suzanne stood across the room talking to a tall man

whose back was toward Callie. He wore a business suit, unusual during the casual summer months in Rocky Point. This time of year tourists out numbered the residents almost five to one.

Callie slowed her pace. Nothing looked like an emergency. Yet the expression on her assistant's face was indescribable. When she spotted Callie, relief became evident.

The man turned.

Callie stopped–totally stunned. Her heart caught in her throat then began to race. For a moment she forgot to breathe.

It was impossible.

Before her stood Tommy Warren!

A thrill of gladness swept through her for a split second. Then the truth hit. This couldn't be Tommy. She'd attended his funeral three months ago.

"Callie Miller?" the man asked.

The voice wasn't Tommy's. It sounded different, more clipped, not lazy and teasing. The expression on his face was mingled: wariness and cynicism. Yet he looked exactly like Tommy.

"Yes?"

"You own this gallery?" he asked.

"I do."

"I thought it belonged to Randolph Artemis."

"It did. He died a couple of years ago. Now it's mine."

No need to go into the details of her inheritance. She'd worked for Randolph for several years, learned so much from him. She missed him every day. He knew she loved the place as much as he had and, with no children to inherit, he'd made Callie his heir.

She'd been totally shocked when she learned the terms of his will. The gallery had been opened decades ago when Randolph had first moved to Rocky Point. He'd originally worked in Manhattan. His fervent beliefs had been people everywhere loved good art and he set out to prove it with his gallery in a small Maine town.

He'd been proven correct over the years and had been able to garner requests from famous artists and sculptors alike to display their work in his gallery. Despite the limited customer base, the gallery flourished.

"He's Tommy's brother," Suzanne said needlessly.

This man was Tommy's identical twin brother.

Chalk it up to something else she'd never learned from Tommy. He never mentioned his younger brother was his identical twin.

Callie started to say that, but closed her mouth.

Why should she be surprised to discover her former fiance's brother was a twin? It wasn't the first thing Tommy kept from her.

Not that it mattered now.

Once again a hint of sadness swept through her. Once upon a time, she'd loved him. In the early days of their relationship, she thought Tommy had hung the moon as they say.

Until that fateful day when she discovered the truth.

She rubbed her chest—the ache as fresh as it had been

three months ago when she'd learned first hand of Tommy's deception and betrayal.

"What can I do for you?" Callie asked, realizing how stupid the question was. Chalk it up to shock at seeing the spitting image of Tommy. She should have offered condolences for his loss.

Studying the man, she realized he didn't quite look exactly like his brother. It was more like seeing a slightly skewed version of Tommy. This man was the same size and shape, but his chest was a bit broader, his jaw a bit firmer. There was an assurance about him that never came from Tommy.

The kind of assurance that came from a quiet self-confidence, not arrogance resulting in bravado and posturing. Tommy had been as charming as could be, which allowed him to get away with things other men couldn't. But she now knew it was all false.

Still, that charm had enabled him to sweep her off her feet. She'd never felt so special as when she'd been with Tommy Warren.

"I'm Trace Warren. I've come to pick up my brother's paintings. I understand you have some of them," he said.

"I do. I just got off the phone with your mother, as a matter of fact. We're finalizing details on the retrospective for his work. I'm not sure what you mean you've come to pick up the paintings? I'll be framing them here. Is that a problem?"

"I need to get the paintings appraised for tax purposes. And if they're worth anything, decide if I want to sell them now or later." He glanced at his watch impatiently.

"Sell them?"

Callie didn't understand. Was he expecting some kind of windfall from Tommy's body of work?

"Your mother said she didn't want the paintings sold. She wants to show them to the community as a memorial to Tommy," she explained. Had he spoken with his mother yet?

The problem was Jocelyn wanted to show all of Tommy's paintings. Callie was hard-pressed to pick a dozen or so to fit in the alcove where the display would be. She wasn't turning her entire gallery over to an unknown, and frankly, a mediocre artist.

She glanced at the alcove where the exhibit would be.

Tommy had continually asked her for an exhibit in her gallery from the day he met her. Fully convinced he'd set the art world on fire, he'd been relentless in pushing to have a one-man show.

She'd been equally resistant.

She didn't want to mix business with her personal life. Plus, sad to say, Tommy's work wasn't the high caliber she was used to displaying. Maybe if he'd worked harder at painting, had improved as he worked, she'd have considered it.

Now, it was forever too late. And while his death hadn't improved the paintings, an emotional tribute to a local man was a different aspect. Her gallery's reputation wouldn't take a hit for being kind to a grieving mother.

"Actually, my mother has little say in the matter. I need

to find out what they're worth and then dispose of them—either sell, give away or toss in the trash, whatever's appropriate."

"These are your brother's paintings. You can't just throw them away." His lack of any sentimentality was jarring.

Callie knew the paintings never would be classified as great works, but wasn't there any family loyalty? The two men were twins, for goodness sake. Weren't twins supposed to have a special bond?

He looked down his nose at her obviously not wishing to belabor the subject.

"As it turns out, I can do whatever I wish with them. To everyone's great surprise, including myself, Tommy had a will and named me as executor."

"I've already scheduled the showing. Announcements have been published in all the local papers. The brochures are at the printer's just waiting the final details. Framing's started. You can't halt everything at this stage," as a hint of panic swept through.

Did he have any idea of how much work she'd already put in for this exhibit?

"Then perhaps you and I need to discuss the matter before things proceed any further. I'm only here for a few days. I need to get everything lined up and taken care of before I leave," he said impatiently.

"Your brother died three months ago and you're just showing up now?"

Where had he been? Why now just days before the scheduled event did he decide to arrive in Rocky Point?

No one had said a word about Tommy's brother at the funeral. She'd thought it odd he hadn't attended, but her own grief and guilt kept her from questioning anything too closely.

Jocelyn was definite with her plans. She wanted her son to have his day in the sun, even if posthumously. Surely as Tommy's brother, and son of Jocelyn, Trace would let the showing proceed.

He glanced at Suzanne, then back at Callie. "Is there some place we can discuss this in private?"

Callie noted that Suzanne hadn't moved an inch. She was taking in everything. While Callie knew she was discrete, he was right. Gallery business should not be conducted in public.

Callie hesitated. She felt like she was in a time warp, talking to Tommy, only not Tommy. Staring at the exact image of Tommy and seeing someone who looked like him but was totally different. Feeling mingled—longing for what was long gone; confusion as she noted the differences between the identical looking men. A little animosity flared at his attitude and his talk about disposing of the paintings which would wreak havoc to her carefully planned show.

An acute awareness of the man's masculinity surprised her.

He was obviously Tommy's identical twin, but neither Tommy nor his parents had ever mentioned that fact to her. All Tommy had ever said was his younger brother rarely came home. How much younger could a twin be?

"Are you the black sheep of the family or something?"

she blurted out.

Jocelyn and Montgomery Warren had scarcely ever mentioned this son. Once Jocelyn had said he'd gone off to do his own thing and turned his back on his family. He wasn't interested in painting or sculpting.

From what Callie knew of the family, that made sense. They appeared to have no interest in anything that did not center around art.

"If you call getting a good education and then supporting myself by working, then yeah, I guess you could say that," he replied, amusement dancing in his eyes.

That expression really reminded her of Tommy. Most of their time together, he'd seemed amused. His fun-loving attitude toward life had attracted her from the beginning.

Trace's life seemed to have followed an entirely different path than his brother. Tommy had dropped out of college his first year to paint. The call of his muse, he'd often said.

And paint he did—when the mood struck. The rest of the time, he spent on other pursuits. But none that entailed a nine-to-five job. He usually sought inspiration by lying on the beach, or sailing or drinking.

Their mother, Jocelyn Warren, was a renowned painter. Her works sold for tens of thousands of dollars. Montgomery Warren, the father of the Warren men, an extraordinary sculptor whose marble and granite creations she'd love to represent, but who had an exclusive deal with a Manhattan gallery.

Jocelyn did condescend to sell some of her smaller paintings through Callie's gallery, not as many as Callie might wish for, but probably more than she should expect given how limited her clientele was compared to Manhattan.

Their relationship was a carry over from when Randolph owned the gallery. He'd wooed Jocelyn when she first moved to Rocky Point many years ago.

From the first moment Callie met Tommy, she'd known Jocelyn expected her son to follow in her footsteps. He'd mentioned that often. Yet, not for her precious son the struggles of a starving artist. Jocelyn supplied the cottage he lived in and support while he painted. Even the flashy car that he'd wrapped around a very unforgiving tree had come from his mother.

Tommy had painted, partied and left a collection of work—some of which Callie was going to show in memory of a man who died too young.

Now this man, Tommy's own brother, threatened those plans. She needed to talk to him and he was right, the showroom wasn't the place.

Chapter Two

"Come with me. Suzanne, please handle anything that comes up, will you?"

Callie headed for the workshop in the back of the gallery, where Tommy's paintings awaited framing. The warehouse space was lined with shelves holding different paintings or sculptures. Some were awaiting display. Others had been bought and would be shipped to their new owners in the next day or two.

Frames leaned against one wall, an assortment of sizes and styles used to enhance any work she displayed to make it more appealing to the buyer. Some frames were for sale, others were merely for display use while a painting was on exhibit.

Callie held open the door while Trace Warren stepped inside and looked around. She followed and closed the door to the gallery, leaning against it. She wasn't sure what to expect. Certainly not the image of Tommy now looking at her with impatience.

Tommy would have tried to sweet-talk her into whatever scheme he'd come up with. At one time kisses would have gone a long way to making her fall in with his plans.

For a moment, she missed the love they'd shared—that she'd thought they'd shared.

This man looked coldly around the space and didn't say a word. She refused to take offense, though she could feel herself bristle a little in defense of her workshop. But there'd be no cajoling, no teasing, no kisses. He looked hard as iron.

"I understand you were Tommy's fiancee," he said, studying her from head to toe.

She felt like a display piece. One he didn't wish to purchase.

She nodded watching him warily.

For a moment she felt a pang that she hadn't known he was a twin. How awful to be part of a family who disregarded him so completely. She'd scarcely heard his name in all the time she'd spent with Tommy and his parents.

He didn't fit her idea of a black sheep. He looked dynamic and successful.

She had a good eye for fine things and the suit and shoes he wore were fine indeed. His hair was cut shorter than Tommy's and his eyes were clear and sharp.

She took a breath in surprise when that smidge of interest didn't quickly dissipate. It was totally unwanted. He wasn't Tommy. And she wouldn't have any interest if he were. Tommy had seen to that.

She shook off the momentary lapse. She'd had enough dealings with the Warrens. The sooner this one was gone, the better.

"We were engaged," she acknowledged. "He told me

once he had a brother who was off building bridges. Since he never mentioned another brother, I assume that's you."

"It's probably all he told you. I'm an engineer, and yes, I build bridges in places of the world where transportation means the difference between living and dying for entire villages."

"So far off the grid you didn't know he died before now?" she asked.

"Pretty much. The message about his death didn't reach me until last week. It's taken me this long to get here."

"Last week? He died three months ago. Your office didn't find a way to notify you sooner?"

She found that impossible to believe. With modern technology of e-mails and texts, surely some notification could have made it through earlier than last week.

Despite not wanting to feel anything for the man, she felt a touch of regret that he'd just learned of his brother's death.

"Do you know my parents well?" Trace asked.

"I've known them for several years. Primarily your mother. She sells some of her work here. I do have to say I don't know her very well."

She wouldn't tell him how Jocelyn was driving her crazy ever since the accident about the showing of Tommy's work. She was Trace's mother, as well, and Callie believed in being discreet.

Wasn't that the reason she never told what she'd discovered the last day she saw Tommy? She wanted to spare Jocelyn the heartache.

And herself the embarrassment, if she were honest.

She wished she'd never known. She wished that Tommy had gone to his grave with the secret and she could mourn him with all the passion she once held for him.

"My mother called the home office and left word for me to call. Nothing more. Nothing to indicate that it was a family emergency, not that there had been a death in the family. The message about the call came in my regular mail, which I get about every three to four months, unless it's critical, in which case it gets faxed or flown in."

From the tight control he exercised, she suspected he was furious with the situation. She'd always heard twins had a close connection. How sad to lose his brother and then not find out for three months. Surely Jocelyn wouldn't have done it deliberately.

The woman lived in her own world, however. Surfacing occasionally to interact with others, then going back to being caught up in the paintings she did so brilliantly. Callie suspected Jocelyn had no idea of the isolation of her other son.

"So when I returned her call last week, she told me the news," he ended bleakly.

"I'm so sorry," she said, her heart going out to him. Despite everything, she'd loved Tommy once. She could relate to how his brother must be feeling at the loss of his sibling.

He ignored her offer of sympathy. "Where are the paintings?"

She went to the rack where she had them stacked. To an

outsider, it might look haphazardly arranged, but she knew exactly where everything was.

The large room was climate controlled, necessary in the salty air of Rocky Point and the humidity of summer. Tommy's paintings were arranged by subject matter. She gestured to the facing one. A sea scene depicting the rugged rocky coast viewed from some of the bluffs around town.

Trace studied it a moment, then looked at her.

"What's its value?"

Was that all he cared about? Money?

"I haven't appraised the lot. Your mother said she only wanted them on display, not appraised for an asking sale price."

"My mother lives in her own world. What price would you list it for in the show?"

"Actually the show is a retrospective. Your parents didn't plan to sell any paintings. I thought your mother wished to keep his work."

He reached into an inner coat pocket and pulled out a bulging envelope. He held it out for her.

"You'll see Tommy left me in charge of his estate. According to his attorney, I have complete authority. And I don't have time to wait around for several weeks while you show his paintings and then decide what the next step is. I have a bridge halfway built. I want to liquidate the assets and divide them among the family members as he indicated. Then I need to get back to work."

Callie took the envelope and then looked at him.

"Leave the paintings in my hands and I'll let you know

how the showing goes," she said flippantly. "Your mother really wants to honor Tommy's memory."

Callie hoped hosting the exhibit would ease some of her own regret at the way things turned out.

Trace studied the painting for a minute. "Is it any good?"

Callie looked at it unsure exactly how to respond.

"It will appeal to a certain portion of the population," she said carefully.

"Like some farmer in Iowa?" he said derisively.

She looked at him in surprise. Did he know she was from Iowa? Was that a criticism on her judgment? She grew a little annoyed.

He picked up on it.

"Hey, I may not be an artist, but I do know artistic values. I can recognize excellent work. My mother's paintings have a depth that's amazing and a use of color that's phenomenal. This looks like a paint-by-numbers view of an ubiquitous seascape," he continued.

Callie bit her lip in indecision. Normally she agreed with customers–it went a long way to selling art. Agreement with the artists kept them happy and kept them bringing in more work. She didn't like confrontation. But this was different.

"Am I wrong?" he challenged. His dark eyes so like yet unlike Tommy's, held hers.

"No," she admitted reluctantly. "But there's a definite market from tourists who want souvenirs to remind them of their vacation."

"So why a show? If they aren't any good, let's get rid of them. I think they'd be more suited to the harbor tourist traps than a reputable gallery like this one."

"I didn't say they weren't any good. Your mother wanted to have a showing of some of his paintings. There are so many other galleries she could choose to represent her work, but she chose this one. It's the least I can do to keep a profitable artist interested in continuing to sell her work through my gallery."

And maybe holding the showing would assuage some of her own guilt. Would things have turned out differently if she'd given Tommy a one-man show like he'd asked?

"So you're doing this for my mother?" Trace clarified.

"Primarily."

"What happened at his showing last winter?" Trace asked.

"What showing last winter?" she asked.

A sinking feeling swamped her, remembering Tommy's obsession for a show. Had Tommy turned elsewhere? Maybe another gallery owner had found something in his work she'd missed.

She looked at the picture, searching for an elusive aspect that would change its value.

"He said he was going to have a one-man show, said he'd invite me to the gala event. It pays to have connections in the art world, as I recalled the letter went. When no invitation came, I assumed he'd just forgotten or the invitation would arrive too late to do anything about it. Not that I could have come. I was in Brazil at the time."

"He didn't have a show that I know of," Callie said, remembering how relentlessly he'd pushed for the chance.

But he hadn't wanted an alcove at the gallery when she'd halfheartedly suggested that compromise. Tommy had wanted to commandeer the entire showroom in a solo production.

Tommy's assessment of his work differed from Callie's.

"You'd know–it was this gallery he was talking about," Trace said.

She turned back to the large table in the center of the room. Trace followed her with his eyes.

Callie was in the middle of a family dynamics she didn't want to be involved with. She didn't know all the ins and outs, but this man was not the beloved son Tommy had been. Was there going to be a fight about Tommy's estate?

Nothing was as it seemed. She wished not for the first time that she'd never met Tommy Warren. Never fallen in love with the man. Never discovered him in bed with that beautiful woman.

"Tommy wanted to have an exclusive one-man show with no other paintings or sculptures to compete with. I couldn't do that. It never went any farther than discussions. I'm sorry if he thought otherwise."

She'd known he'd never been happy with her decision. He'd constantly pushed to have her display his work; and she'd constantly refused.

"When were you two going to get married?" Trace asked abruptly.

"Ah, we never set a date," she said shortly. "Why?"

"For a grieving almost-wife, you seem fairly complacent about his death," he commented.

"For me it happened three months ago, you're the one who just learned about it," she said. "I don't wish to get in the middle of a family argument. Your mother and father asked me to do this. If, as executor of the estate, you say no, of course I'll comply. But you need to be the one to inform your mother."

Callie thought of all the different things she'd have to deal with to stop a show at this stage. The caterer would be all right. Marcie was a friend and could always use the food in the restaurant she owned.

Callie would have to just write off the pre-publicity expenses.

Maybe she could get the printer to cut her a break. She used him exclusively, so maybe he'd be generous and not charge her for the time he'd already spent drafting the program. It hadn't gone to press yet.

Trace turned back to the paintings, pulling the first one forward so he could see the next one, and the next. Soon he'd looked at every one she'd selected.

"This all?"

"All I'm planning to show. I've allocated the alcove to the left for Tommy's work. Your mother isn't pleased with it, but it's the best I can offer."

"He had more?"

"Of course. As far as I know he never sold a single one. He has stacks of canvasses at the cottage. I chose the ones that I thought best represented his work."

And had the most chance for a sale in case Jocelyn changed her mind.

"My mother didn't choose these?" Trace asked, replacing them against the wall.

"She can't bring herself to look at them yet. She trusts me to do the best for him."

Callie wondered if Jocelyn would continue in that trust if she ever learned Callie had broken the engagement two days before Tommy died.

She looked away, remembering.

It'd be a long time before she'd forget that betrayal. She'd loved him and he'd thrown that away. But to keep his mother from knowing the situation after Tommy's death, Callie hadn't told anyone but her best friend. She didn't think the distraught mother could cope with more at this point.

"Has she ever seen his work?" Trace asked.

"I suppose so. Why wouldn't she have seen what he was doing over the years?"

Callie had never questioned that. The dinners she'd attended with the family had focused on discussion about works in progress. Tommy always had a good story about what he was working on.

Had Jocelyn seen his recent paintings? Or any for that matter?

"My mother knows talent. There is very little showing here."

"Maybe as a mother, she thinks everything her sons do is perfect," Callie said, wondering not for the first time what Jocelyn's reactions would be when she saw the paintings hanging from the gallery walls. To hear her talk, Tommy had extraordinary talent.

She was going to be so disappointed.

Callie had asked her several times to come look at the paintings. Jocelyn steadfastly refused.

"Not all sons," he said absently. "Can you give me an appraisal for tax purposes? Not just of these, but of all he did?"

Callie nodded slowly. She could do a formal appraisal. She'd done it before and her credentials gave her the expertise to be accepted by the IRS. However, she wasn't sure she wanted to.

She was trying to forget Tommy and move on with her life. What would being surrounded by his paintings, visiting the cottage where she'd been so happy and so devastated, do to her equilibrium?

"I'm heading to his cottage next. How many canvasses will I find there?"

"Lots. I never inventoried or counted. He has them stacked against the walls of his studio."

Trace glanced at his watch. "Have you had lunch yet?"

Surprised at the question she shook her head.

"Come eat with me and tell me what I need to know about art and how it's appraised and how much it'll cost for the appraisal and how long the appraisal process will take," Trace said.

Callie thought it sounded more like an order.

"There're other appraisers around. Maybe you should get one of them."

She didn't want to go back to the cottage.

"Conflict of interest?"

"I'd give you an honest assessment. But you might wish for someone else."

Would she truly give a reliable, unbiased appraisal or would the hurt and anguish of the last few months color her assessment?

No, where art was concerned, nothing stood in the way of her honest and forthright opinion.

"You know his work. You'd be best."

Trace's attention focused on her. Those dark eyes seemed to peer deep into her innermost part. Her breath caught for a moment. She felt a warmth and curiosity that surprised her. What was there about this man that caught her unaware? He was grieving for his brother. That should give them a common bond. She grieved for Tommy's death. And for the lost love she'd so happily embraced.

Callie blinked. She could almost feel energy radiating from Trace. His focus on her was unsettling. He wasn't at all like Tommy despite his looks. She'd do well not to confuse the two just because they looked identical.

"I'm pretty busy now or will be if the showing goes forward," she said, stalling.

She didn't want to spend any more time with Trace Warren than absolutely necessary. Or with the bittersweet memories of Tommy from when he first began courting her.

"But you know art values," he clarified.

She nodded.

"You don't want my parents to know everything is worthless, is that it? They'll blame you if you don't appraise it high? And that would damage your relationship with my mother, who's probably a very profitable artist for your gallery," Trace guessed.

She shook her head. "I never said Tommy's paintings are worthless. They're not up to your mother's standards. She thinks he was tremendously talented. I hate to be the one to disappoint her. I like your mother." Most of the time.

"Don't worry about Mom. Where art's concerned, she's ruthlessly honest."

Callie was trying to gradually pull back from Jocelyn and Montgomery and their grief. She longed for the business relationship she'd enjoyed when Randolph had still been alive and running the gallery. Before Tommy had swept her off her feet. Before things had gone so wrong and emotions and relationships became tangled.

She studied the man in front of her another minute. He looked so much like Tommy she had to keep reminding herself he wasn't. If he kept looking at her, she'd forget business decorum and reach out to touch him.

Once burned, twice shy was the old saying. She needed to be more cautious in her personal life from now on. Not take at face value words designed to convince her she was special. This man was yummy to look at, but was he any different from his brother on the inside?

"It's only lunch," he said, amusement creeping into his eyes.

Her bones felt as though they were melting. That look was captivating. She turned away, trying to get control. This was not Tommy. And if he were, she'd be furious with him.

"Come and fill me in. We can visit the cottage afterward

and you can give me an estimate on time and cost for an appraisal."

His tone was almost cajoling. Maybe he also had some of that charm that Tommy displayed.

She needed to think this through. On the one hand, it was merely business. She could assess the paintings, do a written report and add some funds to her coffers with her fee. She could handle that.

On the other hand, the man was a constant, vivid reminder of Tommy. Her emotions were still in turmoil. Could she forget the past and do the work without some emotional cost?

And without becoming infatuated with the spitting image of the man she'd thought she'd loved until three months ago?

She turned toward the door.

"All right. I need to get my purse and let Suzanne know I'll be gone for lunch. But I can't go to the cottage this afternoon, I have an appointment at two."

She'd take this one step at a time. If she could manage lunch with Trace, it would give her an idea of how working with him might be.

"So we'll discuss when you can schedule the appraisal over lunch. Get your purse, I want to look at the rest of these paintings."

He turned his attention back to the canvasses stacked in the rack.

Callie had a feeling she was making a mistake. She still held the envelope he'd given her. Maybe she could quickly read through the papers to make sure Trace was who he said he was. She couldn't imagine agreeing to his demands and finding out later it was all false.

As she walked through the display area to return to her office, she was pleased to notice several people browsing. Suzanne stood by attentively, yet let them gaze at whatever they wanted without interrupting them. The gallery was located right on Harbor Street, a main thoroughfare of Rocky Point. The colorful historic town was a tourist Mecca in the summer months. Randolph had opened the gallery decades ago, before the current interest in historic getaways swept the monied set. It was the best location in town situated near an antique shop and a couple of blocks down from the cafe.

Once inside her office, Callie opened the envelope. Inside was a copy of Tommy's will. She hadn't been at the reading as he'd left her nothing having written the will long before he met her. But Jocelyn and Hamilton had been there. Neither one mentioned Trace was the executor.

She'd been surprised to learn that Tommy even had a will. It seemed in direct contrast to his happy-go-lucky nature.

The will was short and to the point. He requested his estate be liquidated and the money divided between his parents and his brother, except for whatever paintings his brother might want. And he actually had appointed Trace as executor.

"Probably because he's the only one in the family who isn't the temperamental, artistic type," she murmured.

The accompanying letter from the attorney outlined Trace's duties and authority. Trace Warren was the man to deal with, not Jocelyn or Montgomery. And even if they wished to keep the paintings, they couldn't. They'd have to purchase them from the estate. How ironic.

Callie reached into the drawer for her purse wondering how this would complicate her life. Nothing was ever the way it seemed when dealing with the Warrens.

Chapter Three

Trace stood near one of the large plate-glass windows at the front of the gallery gazing out over the busy street when Callie finally left her office. He felt as if he were in some kind of time warp. His parents hadn't been overjoyed to see him. His mother accused him of deliberately staying away from the funeral. He'd explained about the timing of the message, but she refused to accept any responsibility on its delay, saying she'd told the woman who answered to have him call. It was more trouble than it was worth to keep repeating she should have mentioned it was a family emergency.

Sometimes he wondered how his mother made it in the real world. She expected everything to run according to her rules and when they didn't, it was never her fault.

Being an artist was the cause. She milked that mystique for all it was worth.

Trace remembered making meals when he was in high school so the entire family could eat. His mother would be lost in painting, his father engrossed in his studio. Tommy had either been out with some girl or talking on the phone.

How did they manage meals now, he wondered briefly.

"I'm ready," Callie said, coming to stand next to him.

He glanced at the woman his brother had been going to marry. He didn't understand this relationship, either. Callie was not the type of woman he knew Tommy liked. She didn't have big white-blond hair, wasn't built like a Playboy bunny and seemed all-around stable.

Her honey-golden hair barely brushed her shoulders. Her blue eyes held honest appraisal when she looked at him. She wore little makeup. Her dress was suitable for a successful businesswoman. Had his brother finally given up his bimbos and settled down with someone who could add stability to his life?

Or had he proposed to insure he always had a gallery to display his painting?

The cynical thought wasn't fair to Callie. She was a pretty woman, as well as being a competent business owner. The gallery was obviously doing well.

Maybe his brother had finally matured and been ready to settle down. Trace hadn't seen him in five years. A man could change in that time. Maybe love was the key factor here. He'd heard love could change the world.

"Where do you recommend we eat?" he asked.

"My friend Marcie has a café a couple of blocks up the street. The food's great and the portions are generous. Plus we can walk," she said. "Unless you have another place in mind?"

"No. I don't know the area. My folks moved here when I was in college. I've been here for only a few short visits since then."

"Few and far between, I guess."

Trace opened the large glass door for her and followed her into the sunshine. The wide sidewalks weren't too crowded despite the number of people strolling along. It was late June, the beginning of the summer months when tourists outnumbered the residents five to one. The summer economy kept the town going year-round, but the visits he'd made had all been in fall.

He liked the place better when it wasn't so crowded.

He looked at her. "Didn't Tommy tell you when our parents moved here?"

She kept her gaze forward and shook her head quickly.

"I knew your family was a fairly recent transplant as Rocky Point families go. But they were here before me, so they seemed like longtime residents to me. Tommy wasn't much for talking about the past. He was always looking toward the future and what success he'd achieve when his painting took off."

Or he'd talk about love. The hours they spent together were for the two of them, not talking about his family or the past.

"He was thirty-two years old, how long before his painting took off?" Trace asked.

Callie shrugged. She slipped dark glasses over her eyes. She didn't want to talk about Tommy.

Trace tried not to let it bother him that his brother hadn't shared more information about their family with Callie. He began to wonder what kind of engagement it had been. How could she agree to marry him and not know more about the Warrens?

"How long were you two engaged?" he asked.

"We were engaged for two months," she said.

"And you knew him how long before that?"

She glanced up at him, her expression hard to read with the dark glasses. "Is that important?"

"Just curious."

"Tommy swept me off my feet and we got engaged only a couple of months after meeting. I've known your mother for longer, of course. Randolph represented some of her work so I knew her first from business."

"So how did you two meet?"

He wasn't surprised to hear Tommy had swept her off her feet. He had that ability.

Trace knew he'd never sweep anyone off their feet. He didn't have the glib charm that Tommy displayed so easily.

For him life was more serious. He didn't think the world owed him anything. He had to make his own way. A slight, but significant difference between the two of them.

Women liked the carefree charm of his brother. There'd been plenty of instances in high school and college. He was nothing like Tommy in that area. The few women he'd dated over the last decade had been casual friends. His work in foreign countries didn't make for long-term relationships.

"He came into the shop about a year and a half after I became the owner. He brought a painting to show me, wanting me to represent him. I declined based on the one painting, but he was persistent, insisted on taking me to dinner to discuss things. We began dating and before long he asked me to marry him. I said yes."

She kept her eyes forward, not wanting to give any clue to her feelings. And they were all over the place. She'd been crazy to say yes after so short a time. Tommy made her feel so alive, so cherished. A more prudent move would have been to wait. Nothing could change the past. She'd said yes and that had started the engagement.

Where was the falling-in-love part? Trace wondered. Maybe Callie was still too raw from Tommy's death to talk about that.

Yet there was a hint of anger in her tone. Wasn't that part of the grieving process, anger that the person who died had left?

"You two were obviously not very close," she commented.

"Distances prevented it."

Distance and their past. Trace kept secrets few people knew he had. Tommy had moved on, why couldn't he?

"With today's e-mail and cell phones everywhere, you could have kept in closer contact if you both wanted. I always thought twins were close," she said.

"Maybe ones who share more than just looks. I don't have the family artistic talent. Tommy couldn't care less about load ratios and wind factors. He went his way and I went mine."

"And never the two shall meet," she finished. "I didn't even know you were twins," she said sadly.

Trace looked at her in surprise. "Tommy didn't speak of me at all?"

"Only to say you were the younger brother and worked out of the country and the family rarely saw you. Which explained why you weren't at home for Christmas."

Trace didn't want it to bother him, but it did. How could his brother be so close to this woman and not even mention they were twins? He'd never fully understood Tommy. This was another incident to add to the list.

They reached the café and entered. Trace noted how full it was, with only a couple of empty tables in the entire establishment. The waitresses were dressed in colonial attire, the place gave a warm and friendly vibe. He knew tourists loved it.

Outside, he saw a huge wooden deck, dotted with umbrellas to shade the tables--most of which were full of laughing, happy tourists and townsfolk eating lunch.

"Inside or out?" the hostess asked.

Trace looked at Callie and she said outside.

He nodded and the hostess led them to one of the umbrella-shaded spots near the railing. The air was calm today, with only an occasional gentle gust of wind. A perfect June afternoon in Rocky Point.

Trace saw several people look their way as they walked through the crowd and do a double-take. They'd probably known Tommy. Had they also not known Tommy had a twin?

He felt overdressed in his suit. Everyone on the deck was in casual shorts and cropped shirts. Dark glasses repelled the sun's glare. His suit was as out of place here as at the bridge site.

As soon as he returned to the Rocky Point Inn, where he was staying, he'd change into something more casual.

It'd been a long time since he'd taken a vacation. He'd planned to combine the business of Tommy's estate with some time relaxing in the seaside town. Working in the jungle he wore khakis and the coolest cotton he could. Those clothes would fit in here, as well, he thought, surveying the other men.

He looked at Callie. Her dress was pale pink and looked cool, sort of casual, yet businesslike. Her hair blew away from her face which left it available to his gaze. Her skin was lightly tanned, her dark glasses hiding her eyes from his.

He wondered what she thought about dealing with him now, instead of his mother.

He'd already run into trouble with his mom on the terms of Tommy's will. She didn't approve of Trace's having the control and claimed she should have all of Tommy's paintings.

It was a formality only; if she wanted them, she could buy them all. The money went into the estate and then it would be divided back between him and his parents.

Still, he planned to follow the letter of the will. Tommy had obviously written it for a reason.

Trace recalled his surprise to get a call from the lawyer once he'd spoken to his mother. He hadn't known Tommy had named him executor. Heck, he hadn't even known Tommy had written a will.

Everything with the estate had been put on hold until Trace could be located. How long would it take to wrap everything up?

He and Callie both ordered the shrimp subs and iced tea. The hum of many conversations provided a background white noise. The erratic breeze from the sea kept the temperature manageable, though Trace did slip off the suit jacket and roll back his shirt sleeves.

"It's getting hotter. Not many men wear suits here," she commented.

"I came straight from the airport. I saw my parents briefly then came to see you," he explained.

Now he wished he'd changed first. He felt like a fish out of water here. Still, he was on a short time frame and was impatient to get things going. He wanted to wind up the estate and get back to work. His second in command could handle things, but Trace liked to run the construction site himself.

"I read the will," she said. "It appears you have full authority. How does that impact the show? Will you let it proceed?"

She withdrew the envelope from her purse and handed it back to him.

"I knew nothing about the proposed show. When I discussed handling the estate with the lawyer who wrote the will, we made plans to liquidate assets as quickly as possible. We're already three months after his death. My mother can buy his pictures, based on your appraisals, and show them if she wishes. If his paintings weren't selling, what was he doing for money?"

Callie didn't know how much his family talked to each

other. Not much if Trace's questions were anything to go by. She was curious about the true relationship. Tommy had said so little about his brother, or anything else actually–except how fabulously they'd live once his paintings sold.

And how much he loved her. How he would treat her like a queen when the money began to roll in.

Foolish pipe dreams she now knew better than to believe. Her face flushed in memories of the love she thought they'd shared.

How could she never have asked questions, always been content to bask in the moment. She'd been an idiot in retrospect. But what a blissful few weeks she'd experienced. Too bad they'd been totally false.

Trace was watching her. Had he said something?

"How did Tommy live?" he repeated.

"Your mother subsidized him. He kept saying he'd pay her back once he began to sell."

She tried to keep her tone neutral. Her parents lived a modest lifestyle in Iowa. She'd been raised to become self-sufficient at a young age. She couldn't imagine her own parents thinking they had to support her at this point in her life.

She looked away.

That was unfair. They would help her in a heartbeat if she'd really needed it.

Jocelyn had lots of money; she probably didn't think two thoughts about subsidizing Tommy.

"He was thirty-two years old and hadn't begun to earn a living. Would he really ever have?" Trace asked.

She bit her lip, feeling the wash of guilt.

Would it have hurt her to have displayed one or two of his paintings in her gallery? Maybe some tourist would have bought them and given Tommy a boost that could have changed his future.

"It's hard to say." Because she hadn't given him that chance.

She looked at Trace, feeling surreal talking to the man who looked so like Tommy. His features were so alike to be disturbing. Only the shorter haircut and different attitude showed her she wasn't living in some dream or caught up in the past.

She could be excused for the awareness that hovered. He looked like someone she'd once loved. Her body had a hard time differentiating between them.

But her mind knew. She wasn't going down that idyllic dream path a second time.

Their sandwiches came and for a moment conversation was suspended while they began to eat.

"Tell me about yourself," Trace said a little later. "You're not from here–I can tell from your accent."

She laughed and put down the sandwich she was about to take another bite from.

"I like to think I have no accent and those from here are the ones with the definite accent. I'm from Iowa. I went to college in Boston, studied fine arts, then looked for the ideal job. I found a less than ideal one in Boston but took it so I had the opportunity to learn all I could about current art, appraising, marketing. I spent weekends and vacations looking for another position. A few years ago I came to Rocky Point for a long weekend, fell in love with the place and began to look for a job. Randolph Artemis was kind enough to hire me and here I've been ever since."

"It's a nice town, what little I've seen over the years. My parents lived in Boston until I started college. I've been on my own since, and for the most part on assignments out of the country, so I've never spent much time here. But I remember my mother raving about Randolph's gallery. It was one of the best in all of New England, she once said."

"I like to think it still is. He died almost two years ago. I was fortunate he left the business to me," she said quietly.

He raised an eyebrow at that but before he could speak, he heard a rise in the conversation level. Turning, he saw his mother winding her way through the tables, her angry gaze fixed on him.

Chapter Four

Jocelyn Warren made her way through the tables until she stopped at theirs.

"What are you doing talking to Callie?" she demanded, frowning at her son.

Trace rose politely. "I didn't expect you to join us for lunch," he said easily.

"I'm not joining you! I stopped by the gallery and Suzanne said you'd taken Callie to lunch. Knowing Callie and Marcie are friends I took a chance you'd be here. What's going on?"

She glared at Callie. "Trace is nothing like Tommy. He's only here to wreak havoc with our lives."

Trace was glad to see some things never changed–like his mother's bent for dramatics.

Turning back to her son, she continued, "Haven't we had enough heartache with Tommy's death without your interfering with our plans?"

Her dramatic tone seemed to expand to include the entire deck and all the people there. Most of the customers at nearby tables stopped eating, fascinated by the scene unfolding.

"I'm only following Tommy's instructions, Mother. You saw the will, you know this is what he wanted," Trace said quietly.

He knew better than to argue with her. She loved an audience. Did she realize so many people were watching?

"He wrote that will several years ago. Things changed. He should have left me the paintings or at least left them to Callie. She was going to be his wife. It's not fair!"

Callie started to open her mouth, thought better of it and closed it firmly. Glancing around, she saw other customers avidly observing every nuance. Conversation on the deck had stopped completely.

"Jocelyn, please, sit down and join us," she urged. "People are staring."

Jocelyn paused, glanced around haughtily and then sat in the chair Trace quickly drew out for her.

She glowered at her son. "You stay away from Tommy's fiancee. I remember the rivalry you two boys had, always trying to take away each other's girls. He was happy here, away from your interference. Stay away from Callie!"

"Then shall I find someone else to appraise Tommy's paintings? We were having lunch to discuss that," Trace said easily, sitting back in his chair.

He wondered if he was going to be able to finish his sandwich. How did his mother live with such high drama all the time? He found it wearing.

Jocelyn looked surprised. She glanced at Callie.

"Of course I want Callie to appraise his work. She'll do a marvelous job. She loved Tommy and admired his paintings, right dear?"

Callie gave a polite smile but kept quiet, lest she end the months of silence and tell Jocelyn exactly what she'd thought of Tommy, and how she'd ended their engagement forty-eight hours before he crashed his car against that tree.

If and when she told, it would not be at a crowded restaurant with gossipers listening avidly.

Actually, she had no plans to bring more heartbreak to Jocelyn. The woman had loved the idea of their marriage. She'd been needy after her son's death, relying on Callie for several things since then. Her heart ached as Jocelyn's must. She didn't want to cause any problems for the family.

"I would appraise the paintings to the best of my ability," she said simply.

"There!" Jocelyn looked in triumph to Trace. "She's the best for the job."

Trace inclined his head slightly, a smile tugging at his lips. "I'm so glad you approve of my choice."

Callie admired his patience. She drew a deep breath, determined not to get upset with Jocelyn this afternoon. She'd had enough turmoil already this day.

"She's one of the best art dealers in Maine," Jocelyn said.

She looked at what they were eating. "I'll have the shrimp sub, also," she said.

Trace summoned the waitress and placed an order for his mother.

After that Jocelyn virtually ignored Trace to talk to Callie.

"I planned to stop by the gallery to look at that alcove

again. I think it's too small and not light enough for the best display of his paintings."

"Mother," Trace interrupted. "Have you seen the pictures Callie picked out for the show?"

"Not yet." Jocelyn paused a moment, then took a deep breath. "I cannot bring myself to see my darling boy's work. I know I will be devastated all over again. It's all I can do to make it through each day. Planning this retrospective has given me something to focus on. I'm sure opening night will be almost more than I can bear."

For a moment Callie thought Jocelyn might start crying. She'd been inconsolable at the funeral.

Callie had visited Jocelyn and Montgomery a few times since, slowly spacing the visits farther and farther apart.

One day they'd move back into the realm of gallery owner-artist, but for the time being, she was destined to play the part of grieving fiancee.

Half the time she felt like such a fraud. The other half, she genuinely grieved the loss of his life and wished fervently that Tommy Warren were still alive.

And that she'd never walked in on him that afternoon.

"They're not up to your standards," Trace said bluntly.

Jocelyn waved her hands in the air as if that was of no importance. "Probably not yet. I've had twenty years more experience than he had. But the talent was there. Given time, he probably would have been one of the leading painters of the twenty-first century."

Callie blinked. Jocelyn really was living in a fantasy world.

"No," she said involuntarily.

Jocelyn and Trace looked at her.

"What?"

Callie shifted position slightly, glancing at Trace in appeal.

"The paintings are nothing like what you do, Jocelyn. I don't believe Tommy had the discipline you have to continue to grow in his work."

She stopped short. If what Trace said earlier was true, Jocelyn needed to see the paintings before she'd ever believe her precious son would never have achieved her level of success.

Unless he stopped drinking, of course.

Maybe his entire life would have been different had he not wanted to party more than anything.

Why hadn't she realized that at the time? She'd enjoyed their partying as much as he had. But she wouldn't have continued forever.

Would he have settled in marriage? Quiet evenings at home? Preparing a meal together? Sailing on the bay? She'd never know.

In retrospect, they had so little in common.

"Come by the gallery and see them," Callie continued. "Help me choose which frames to use for the different subjects I've chosen. If you don't like them, we have time to select others from his inventory."

"Oh, I couldn't bear it. I don't know how I shall be able to be at the showing, yet for my poor son, I shall be there. But I don't believe I can see them more than once so soon after his death."

"You need to view them before the show," Trace said. "They aren't very good."

"How dare you besmirch your brother's work! From the time he was seven or eight years old, he showed great promise. We all know you have no artistic talent, Trace. Don't belittle what you can't do yourself!"

Trace's eyes narrowed as if in anger. But his voice remained calm when he spoke, "I can't draw worth beans, I know. But I do recognize talent and it's not there."

The waitress arrived with Jocelyn's sandwich.

"Wrap it up, I'm leaving," she said imperiously.

She rose.

Trace rose.

Callie watched bemused as they stared at each other for a long moment. Jocelyn spoke again, "I expect the show to proceed as planned. I trust Callie to have selected the best of his work and once the community sees the paintings, everyone will realize the loss to the art world his death caused. You're the executor, figure out how to have those paintings available for the show."

She followed the waitress back toward the restaurant proper to get her wrapped sandwich.

Trace sat and looked at Callie. "She's heading for a big disappointment."

"The paintings aren't that bad," Callie said diplomatically.

"They aren't that good. She expects to see masterpieces. Instead she's going to see mediocre work. Are those the best?"

Callie nodded, fiddling with her iced tea glass.

"He liked to have a good time, didn't he? He never wanted to be responsible, accountable, or grow up. And there was no need, as long as Mom subsidized him," Trace said with frustration.

Callie said nothing. She began to eat again, but the sandwich tasted like cardboard. As soon as she could, without looking as if she were fleeing, she wanted to leave.

"So when can you come out to do the appraisal?" he asked.

He was relentless.

"Not before Thursday afternoon," she said. Today was Tuesday; if he was in such a rush, maybe he wouldn't want to wait that long.

She again thought it would be better to have another appraiser handle the task. She felt battered from all the drama of the day. She couldn't imagine Jocelyn taking her appraisal lightly.

"Fine. What time?" he asked.

"Two?"

She should have said she was busy until next week or next month. Or just flat out told him no. She glanced at him. She didn't think many people told him no.

"I'll be there. I have to clear out Tommy's things. See if there is anything else worth selling. Most of his clothes I'll donate. Do you have a recommendation where?" Trace asked.

"There's a thrift store in Monkesville–the next town

over–that supports a children's home. If I were donating, I'd donate there."

"What of his things do you want?" he asked gently.

Callie shook her head. "There is not one thing I can think of that I want."

She was truly not entitled to anything, even if Trace thought differently. She'd ended their engagement.

Had her ending the engagement caused Tommy to crash his car? She hoped not, but the nagging doubt remained to haunt her with doubts. He'd been drunk. Had he had more liquor than usual to drown his sorrows in their break up?

She tossed her napkin on the table and rose. "I have to get back to the gallery. Thank you for lunch. I'll see you Thursday at two."

Unless an excuse presented itself before then so she could get out of doing the appraisals without questions being raised, she thought.

Trace rose with her and waited until she walked away before sitting down again.

Just as Callie was about to step away from the deck, she glanced back. He sat gazing out over the back of the deck. For a moment, she thought she caught a glimpse of loneliness.

She hesitated. Maybe she'd misjudged Trace Warren.

There was no denying the tug of her heart as she debated returning to the table.

For what? To see if she could cheer him up? Nothing could do that.

And any close association might lead to a revelation she

didn't want made.

Turning, she headed back to the gallery, already planning how to present her ideas to her next appointment.

And then she'd turn her attention to appraising Tommy's paintings that were currently awaiting framing.

She'd call Jasper Mullins, as well. He owed her a favor and could give a second opinion.

Not that she questioned her judgment. Randolph's instructions over the years and her own experience since gave her confidence in her assessments.

But for what she felt she owed Tommy and his parents, she'd see if she could get another opinion.

Trace stayed at the table long enough to finish his meal. He hadn't eaten regularly in the last couple of days with the time zone changes and three different flights. He was hungry and tired. And not looking forward to winding up his brother's affairs.

He wished things had been different. He loved his mother. He didn't always understand her, but he knew what she considered important. It'd never been about him, always about Tommy. He'd come to terms with that situation years ago.

His father also lived in a dream world most of the time, sculpting from marble or granite—revealing what the rock hid, he always said. He only surfaced when it was time to show the piece. He drove a shrewd deal with his agent and his pieces were now sought after by private collectors as well as modern museums.

The clean salt air felt refreshing after the constant scent

of rotting vegetation that permeated the area around the Amazon River basin. He'd become used to the smell over the months, only now realizing how foul the air seemed in comparison.

Tossing some money on the table, holding his suit jacket with one finger, he slung it across his shoulder and headed back to the Inn. He'd gotten a room there even before visiting his parents when he arrived. He knew he couldn't stand staying with them.

He'd call the office when he reached his room, to let them know he was extending his visit. This estate was not something he could handle in a day or two given the circumstances.

To appease his mother, he'd let the showing take place. He'd have to find out from the attorney how that would affect the probate process.

Once he'd unpacked and changed into cooler clothes, he'd head for the cottage his brother had rented and assess what needed to be done there.

He couldn't believe he'd never see Tommy again. That he wasn't going to be called upon to bail him out of yet another scrape. Or hear some convoluted plan on how Tommy would make a million dollars over night.

They hadn't been close, but he missed him more than he expected.

What had his life been like in Rocky Point? Trace had never visited Tommy here. They'd met in Boston a few years back. And Trace would forever think of him in Boston, not this quaint New England town that catered to tourists.

He wished Tommy had written his will differently.

And if he were wishing, Trace wished he was in the Amazon Basin sweating over delivery of the next supply ship, haranguing the local laborers to work faster or the blasted bridge would never be complete. Wouldn't that have antagonized his mother, to not even come home once he'd learned of Tommy's death?

Yet there was nothing to be done. Tommy was gone. It was hard to grasp he'd never see his brother again. Never find that magic moment when they'd be close as they'd been as young boys, before the obvious favoritism of their parents had caused the schism. Before Tommy had taken advantage of that favoritism and gone wild.

Would they ever have reconnected? Would marriage to Callie have changed him? He'd never know.

Death was very final.

Chapter Five

Callie sat on the sole lounge chair on her minuscule balcony, gazing at the narrow wedge of the sea visible from her third floor flat. The evening was pleasant. She'd put on a baggy T-shirt to sleep in, brought out a glass of white wine and propped her feet on the railing. No one could see her as she sat in the darkness. It was one of her favorite times of the day.

As the ocean breeze cooled the night air, she let her thoughts drift. Time and again they returned to Trace Warren and the ambivalent feelings she had around him. She didn't like him. He reminded her of what she wanted to forget. Yet she felt sadness for his loss. Despite his relationship with his brother, it had to hurt when a sibling died. Callie was an only child, but she could use her imagination.

She knew better than to give into her softer side. Trace wasn't Tommy. A man less needful of someone fussing over him she hadn't met. She'd fallen for Tommy fast and lived to regret it. Could she trust her judgment about men? Especially Warren men?

Yet she wasn't one to sugarcoat things. She'd been

attracted to him. His tanned features looked rugged and masculine. The way he'd looked at her with those dark eyes, as if she was the only thing to focus on, she'd known she had one hundred percent of his attention when he looked at her. She shivered in memory.

Her phone rang. She went inside to get her cell, returning to the balcony as she swiped it on.

"This is Callie," she said, settling down again.

"Is it too late to call?"

She recognized Trace's voice instantly. Suddenly she was fully alert, on edge. Why was he calling?

"Not at all. What can I do for you?"

The darkness hid all things. She could talk to him and keep her secrets.

There was a moment of silence on the other end.

"Trace?"

"This is probably a bad idea," he said.

"What is?"

"Calling to ask you about Tommy. You probably have a million things to do."

"Actually I'm sitting on my balcony enjoying the night air. Where are you?"

"I'm staying at the Rocky Point Inn. One of the last rooms available, so I was told, and lucky to get that, according to the desk clerk. The television has nothing on it to warrant my attention. After eighteen months in Brazil, you'd think I'd have plenty to catch up on, but nothing appeals. I don't know anyone in town except my parents and you. And I guess that's a tenuous connection at best."

"What can I tell you?"

"How he was these last few months? What he was interested in? Besides you, of course. Was he happy?"

She took a sip of her wine, stalling. She didn't want to remember.

"I think Tommy had the capability of being happy no matter what. He never seemed to take anything seriously enough to impact his outlook on life. It was one of the things about him that appealed to me. I worry about the gallery, worry about keeping a steady flow of quality artwork coming in and selling. Worry about taxes and the weather and lots of things. Tommy never did. And when I was with him, I'd forget and have fun."

It was what she missed most about him, she realized.

"Yeah, he had an optimistic outlook that didn't quit," Trace said slowly.

"He used to make me mad sometimes, never thinking the worst could happen. But he was so often right, the worst didn't happen. He had a lot of friends, none close that I know of, but plenty to hang out with, go clubbing, or sailing. He loved being around people--which surprised me a little," she said slowly.

She was again coming to realize some things that should have given her clues to the real Tommy.

"Why's that?"

"Most of the artists I know are content to be their own best friend. Tommy had scads of friends. He wasn't a loner."

"We were different in that aspect. Actually we were different in many ways, not just that. He always seemed to have a flair for making friends. From the time we were in elementary school together, he had a circle of friends for any occasion."

"Did you?"

"I had a few friends. Hung on the outskirts of his groups if I didn't have anyone to hang out with. He was generous that way."

"He was freehanded. I wish—" Callie trailed off.

"What?"

"That I appreciated how he was before he died. I think I wanted him to change, and of course no one can change once they reach a certain age—unless they wish it. I loved his carefree attitude, but wanted him to be more practical. I loved going to parties with him, yet yearned for quiet evenings at home. What does that say about me?"

"That you wanted a balanced life, not all one-sided."

"You make that sound nicer than I think it was."

Not that any of it mattered once she'd discovered him in bed with that woman.

She closed her eyes, wishing she had another memory to supplant that one. It was the worst one she could remember him by.

"You're staying at the Inn?" she said a minute later. "Why aren't you staying at your parents' house? Or at Tommy's cottage? Your mother rents that cottage, you could stay there."

"Let's just say it's easier to come and go if there are no family dynamics to get in the way."

Callie frowned. What did that mean? "Did you get a lot

done today?"

"I went through his clothes, packed them all in bags. There weren't as many ghosts as I expected," Trace said.

"Ghosts?"

"Memories. We were inseparable as boys. We began to go our separate ways in high school and after our first year in college acknowledged we were too far apart in our philosophies of life to keep in close touch. I bet I only saw Tommy a half dozen times in the last decade."

"Your choice or his?" she asked.

Tommy hadn't seemed to miss his brother. Had that been a facade?

There was so much she didn't know about the man she'd once thought she'd marry. Another clue they weren't suited. Why hadn't she picked up on them at the time?

"Mutual." He was silent. "Actually more on my part than his. I was tired of—" He stopped abruptly.

"Tired of what?" she asked.

"Cleaning up after him. It's not important. Water long under the bridge now."

"It's hard to hold on to anger when the person's gone, isn't it?" she said slowly. "He was wonderful at first, then changed a little. Now I'd give anything to have him back— warts and all."

She'd forgiven him for his actions. Tried over and over to understand them. But she knew forgiveness was more for her than Tommy. He hadn't come after her when she'd said they were through.

Couldn't he have told her he had second thoughts? He

could have broken their engagement and moved on, rather than her find them that day.

"Some things seem insignificant after all," Trace said. He took a breath she could hear over the line.

"Changing the subject, what did you do this afternoon?" he asked.

"Instead of coming to the cottage, do you mean?"

"You had plans when I showed up. I was merely curious as to what."

"I met with a client who loves to collect certain glass sculptures. She and I have been working together from the time I first joined Randolph. She's a lovely elderly lady who has enough money to indulge herself."

"Did you sell her anything?"

"Not today. I had nothing I thought suitable for her. But we had a lovely tea and I promised to keep my eye out for just the perfect statue."

"That all?"

"There's more to running an art gallery than sitting around and waiting for people to wander in and buy," she said. Did he think she didn't work hard at her job?

"I didn't mean that. As I said, just curious. Sometime you'll have to tell me all that's involved in running a successful art gallery."

"Maybe sometime I will."

"Tommy's place was dusty. Did he have a maid or something? I can't see my brother cleaning a house. Or am I wrong?"

She smiled, feeling the ache fade. "Actually I can't see

Tommy cleaning house, either. Planning for a blowout party, yes. He had a cleaning service once a week. Maybe your mother suspended the service after his death. I know she hasn't been to the cottage since he died. She's grieving so much it hurts to see her so sad."

"I know. It's going to take her a long time to get over this, if she ever does."

Callie wondered if Trace would ever get over his twin's death. She wished she knew him well enough to ask.

"Do you want me to bring you your things from there? Or will you pick them up on Thursday?" he asked.

Callie felt as if she'd been slapped. She knew there was nothing of hers at Tommy's.

"There's nothing I want," she said slowly.

"Nothing?"

She didn't recognize the odd tone to his voice. Should she have taken whatever was there and not raised questions?

Any feminine apparel had to belong to the other woman.

What a tired cliche. The hurt and betrayal rose again. She was so angry with Tommy she could slap him, if he were still here. How could he lie to her so?

"I want nothing—donate everything. Maybe I should have sorted through the things," she said.

She'd have found anger a driving force to get everything packed up and donated. Anger at herself for being so gullible and falling for a glib charmer. And anger at Tommy for using her and not being honest. Anger that he'd been seeing someone else while professing he loved her. Anger at shattering the dreams she'd built of their future.

Anger that she had not proved to be what he needed as she'd once thought he was what she needed.

"It wasn't that hard. I packed up the clothes from the closet and drawers. The clothes still in the dirty hamper I just tossed. Maybe you can give me the address of the thrift shop and I'll drop them there tomorrow."

Quickly she ran through the things she needed to do the next day. Guilt made her volunteer.

"I could go over with you if you want. It's not hard to find if you know Monkesville, but a bit tricky to give directions as I don't know all the street names, just how to find the place."

"I thought you were busy until Thursday afternoon," he said.

"I said that's when I could start the appraisals. The process takes time and concentration. I have a bit of free time tomorrow afternoon, take it or leave it."

She already regretted her hasty comments. Let Trace find his own thrift shop to donate to.

"I'll take it. I'll take you to dinner afterward in appreciation for your help."

"No need."

She didn't like the fluttering that sprang up at the invitation. This was not some man she could become interested in.

"Take pity on a guy alone in town."

That sparked a laugh. "You are the last man I'd take pity on. Stand on the street corner and six beautiful women will line up to go out with you. I know—Tommy had that effect on women."

She tried hard to keep the bitterness from her voice. She'd been so happy to think he'd chosen her. What a fool she'd been.

"He always did. But you're wrong. I don't have the same effect."

That she did not believe.

"Tell me about your work. How did you get into building bridges instead of painting seascapes?"

She deliberately changed the subject. If he was lonely and wanting to talk, let him talk. He didn't seem comfortable around his parents. With his brother's recent death, he had to be feeling a need to connect with someone. And it was always easier to talk in the dark.

"Twins can look alike externally, but inside our personalities are unique. I like building things."

"Did you ever try to paint?"

"Oh, I tried the whole nine yards, painting, sculpting, music. My parents were determined to find some artistic talent in both their sons. But I gave up after a while and concentrated on what I wanted to do. I didn't have the talent Tommy showed as a kid," Trace said.

"Having talent and developing it are two different things."

"Most artists have a fire inside to do what they do, whether painting, sculpting, writing. I know my folks do. Tommy didn't. I knew him all his life. He didn't have that passion that other artists have. Did that bother you? As a prospective wife, I mean."

Not at first. In the beginning she'd been so in love, so wrapped up in them, she hadn't given his work much notice. It was only after a couple of months, right toward the end–

"Tommy thought he only had to have people see his work and he'd be set for life. It was part of that optimism he had. I'm more pragmatic. So we were yin and yang."

Would it have grown to be a barrier had he not betrayed her so cruelly?

"So why didn't you give him a show?"

Callie was silent for a long time.

"It's very selfish," she said at last, hating to admit the truth. But something about the darkness, about Trace's voice over the telephone line, made it easier to face facts.

"How so?"

"I guard the reputation of the gallery fiercely. He wanted a complete closure of everything but his work. I offered the alcove I'm using now. It wasn't good enough for him. He wanted the entire gallery. I couldn't risk it. My pessimism, I guess. Now I wish I'd pushed harder for a compromise. I so wish he could be at the show, maybe have people love his paintings."

Guilt played a big part. If she'd done more, would he have turned to the other woman?

"You probably think I'm a terrible person to put business before Tommy's wishes," she said evenly.

"Not at all. You have to run your business, not give handouts to anyone who comes along."

Callie suddenly felt as if a weight had lifted.

At least someone knew the truth and didn't condemn

her for it.

Would he feel the same if she told him the entire story? She doubted it. She had a feeling from what Trace had said and done in the short time she'd known him that he was high on loyalty and commitment. And Tommy had been his twin.

"So I'm to go ahead with the show?" Callie asked.

"Go for it. My parents and I'll sort out the legal issues. It means a lot to my mother to see her son's work represented."

"You surprise me."

"Why?"

"Somehow, I think if my parents treated me as yours do you, I wouldn't be as magnanimous."

She shouldn't be saying such things, yet somehow she knew concealed in the darkness that things could be said that wouldn't be uttered in the light of day.

"They're my parents," he said simply.

And you love them, she echoed silently.

Wasn't it macho to admit to such a thing? It sure didn't fit her image of Trace Warren. A tough man in a hard business, he'd surprised her with his dealings with his mother at lunch. She'd expected him to blast the woman for her rudeness. He'd evidenced a lot more patience than she'd expected.

"Tell me how you got into building bridges. Why bridges? Where exactly is this bridge you're building? What's it like there?"

She wanted to know more about this mysterious twin.

"The Amazon Basin is certainly different from Rocky Point. For starters, it's humid and muggy 24/7, with rain as regular as the dawn—only at three every afternoon."

Callie settled in to listen to him describe a world so foreign to hers she was intrigued Trace could so easily travel from one to the other. Time seemed to fly by as he talked about the primitive locale, the untrained locals working with the skilled men from the company he worked for. When he talked about some of the snafus they'd experienced, she laughed. She knew it was hard work, but he had a way of making it sound almost enjoyable.

Her distrust gradually eased. He was a man needed for a difficult task. She could let go some of her trepidation. He wasn't his brother. She needed to remember that.

Nothing would bring Tommy back or give them a second chance. That had passed. She had a new future to forge. But it wouldn't hurt to talk to Trace a little longer.

It was after eleven when Trace said, "I've bored you enough."

"Not at all. You have a way with words. I felt I was right there. I bet you can't wait to get back—heat and humidity and all."

"I like my work but I don't miss the constant heat and insects. Being in Rocky Point's a refreshing change. Short though my break is."

"How long are you staying?"

"Depends on how long all this takes. I'll pick you up at the gallery tomorrow afternoon so you can show me the way to the thrift shop."

"Around four should give us time enough to get there. They close at five."

"Good night, Callie, thanks for listening."

"Thank you, Trace, for the travelogue."

Trace ended the call. He'd been gazing out the window as they'd talked, seeing the lights from a portion of the town, wishing his room had a view of the bay. If he stayed long enough, he'd ask to change when one of those rooms became available.

His room was dark. He needed to get some sleep, but the time zone changes kept him wide awake.

It'd been interesting talking with Callie. He'd felt closer to Tommy when she spoke of their time together. From the sound of things, Tommy had been the same right up to his death. He'd always drawn the women like flies. Flirting with them, he had a knack of making each one feel uniquely special. Had he settled down with Callie?

The most interesting aspect of the entire conversation, however, was the fact she didn't want the women's clothing he'd found at the cottage. She'd sounded odd when he brought it up.

Were they not hers?

If not, then whose? From a long-ago girlfriend?

Or a not-so-long ago girlfriend?

Had Tommy been cheating on the side?

The thought made him sick. Callie was too nice to have his brother treat her so badly.

Trace'd never forget the trouble Tommy got them into at college. Had he continued his predilection for a variety of women even after he'd asked Callie to marry him?

Trace scowled in disgust. It'd be just like Tommy—thinking he was free to do whatever until the marriage vows were exchanged. Or even beyond?

When he thought about it, Trace was constantly amazed that two boys from the same parents, same upbringing, could turn out to view life so differently.

He'd left the feminine apparel out on the bed in Tommy's cottage, thinking it had to belong to Callie, thought the sexy black barely there underwear didn't seem to fit his image of her. But business attire could differ drastically from intimate apparel.

First thing in the morning, he'd bag those clothes and hope the thrift shop just took the bags without opening to inventory the contents while they were there.

Rising, he walked to the open window. The fresh salt breeze blew cool air into the room. The humid, rotten-vegetation air of the jungle was almost forgotten. It'd been a long time since he'd taken much time off from work. He had weeks and weeks of vacation accrued on the books. He'd thought he'd make this trip in a few days, but now wondered if he should stay and see the showing for his brother's paintings. It'd most likely be the only showing given.

He knew Callie was doing it for sentimental reasons and to placate his mother. He'd suspected that from the moment he'd seen Tommy's work.

It wouldn't hurt her business. Most people understood sentimentality, even if they didn't subscribe to it. To dedicate an alcove to honor her dead fiancé's memory was a fine tribute.

He leaned against the window frame and continued to gaze out over the few lights he could see, but his mind was focused on Callie Miller.

He and Tommy had never shared the same taste in women. Before. But this time, he could definitely be interested in the pretty gallery owner. Except—even if she ever returned his regard, how would he know it was him she was thinking of and not Tommy?

A ghost was a powerful thing to compete with-- especially one that looked exactly like him.

There was no room in his life now for complications. He was in Rocky Point to settle his brother's affairs and that was all.

But for the first time ever, he wished he'd seen a certain woman before Tommy had.

Chapter Six

Callie paced the gallery in nervous anticipation. It was almost four o'clock. She kept an eye on the street from the big plate-glass window. The gallery was empty of customers at the moment. Suzanne was at the counter, tallying the day's receipts. For a Wednesday, they'd done well.

"You're going to wear a hole in the carpet," Suzanne murmured.

Callie glanced at her assistant. She had her head bent over the adding machine, but she peeped up at Callie and laughed. "You almost act as if you're going on a date."

"No. I just don't want him to have to hunt for parking. When I see him, I'll zip out and we'll be on our way."

She took a deep breath. Trace was a man on a mission. She wasn't going on a date. But the nerves that jangled could be confused for excited anticipation. She wasn't sure she should be doing this. Yet she was anxious to see him again. After the conversation last night she felt she knew him a little better.

"Right," Suzanne said.

"Really," Callie insisted, knowing she was keyed-up.

Which was silly.

He looked exactly like Tommy. She'd had enough of Tommy's antics. How could she look at Trace and not see his brother? It was confusing. Yet she knew there was a difference. She could feel it, despite the identical faces.

A nondescript white sedan slowed in front of the gallery. She spotted Trace driving.

"Lock up," she told Suzanne as she pulled open the door and hurried outside.

Trace saw her and stopped. Fortunately the traffic behind him didn't seem to mind. She quickly got into the car and he sped away.

"Parking's a bear," he said. "I didn't realize since the Inn has plenty of spaces."

"It's usually easier to walk everywhere than find parking during the summer months. Come November you'll see a completely different side to things."

"Cold, I bet."

"Sure, this is New England. We even get snow."

"Which way do we go?" he asked.

Callie gave directions, gradually relaxing as the scenery sped by. Trace didn't talk much and she kept quiet. It had been easier last evening to talk on the phone.

"Busy day?" he asked as they left the town limits and sped up along the highway. The tall stand of trees gave a rural feel to the road that connected two very busy towns.

"A bit. Wednesdays are the days for special excursions for clubs and groups and today turned out to be one for garden groups from all over the area. We had dozens of women in buying up all the floral paintings and two even asked for future work from one of the artists."

"Do artists come to you or do you go out searching for the next new talent?" he asked.

"Randolph built up a steady list of excellent artists. I try to keep them happy by selling their work. During the winter months, the gallery's closed several days during the week so I can make trips to nearby towns and cities to search for new artists. I have some regulars from as far away as Quebec and Virginia. Most are local to the areas of Maine, Massachusetts and Rhode Island."

"So you combine mini vacations with searching for new talent."

"Yes I guess you could say that."

Callie had been burning with curiosity ever since Trace mentioned the women's clothing last night. What had he done with it? Did he suspect the truth when she'd blurted out they weren't hers?

Maybe the woman she'd discovered in bed with Tommy had not been a one-time deal like he'd said. Would it have mattered if he'd been seeing her longer?

Tommy hadn't taken their breakup well. Had her decision been so hard to take that he'd been careless—drinking to excess and then speeding until he crashed?

She couldn't dwell on that. She'd done what she'd thought was right, what she had to do to keep her own self-respect. She wasn't responsible for Tommy's accident. She'd prayed many nights for the Lord to forgive her of any wrongdoing in relation to Tommy. She felt a peace from the

Lord and even if she never knew for sure if Tommy had been shattered by her breaking the engagement, she was prepared to go on with the thought of forgiveness for his betrayal.

"Turn here and head for the center of town," she said some time later as they approached Monkesville.

The larger town looked similar to Rocky Point. The New England saltbox houses were weathered from the centuries of use. The main street buzzed with activity, giving every evidence of the summer tourism boom. Prim brick shops with old-fashioned signs displayed from the facades blended with some newer buildings made of glass and concrete.

"Turn left here and go up three blocks, then we'll turn left again. Then right and then left. It's on a dead end street," she said, pointing to a street that climbed a slight hill.

Trace drove the short distance, turning into the parking lot of the thrift shop a few moments later. Colorful flags fluttered over the entrance to the shop. The parking lot was half full. He parked and unloaded several bags.

Callie sat in the car, watching him as he gave away his brother's clothes. It had to be hard. She'd been fortunate in her life not to have to deal with death before this. Her grandparents, all four, were alive and well. Her parents were in great health. No friends had yet died.

Only an ex-fiance. And only she knew about the ex part. It would help no one to tell of their breakup and she felt it'd hurt Jocelyn. So Callie kept the secret from all except her best friend.

"All set," Trace said, getting back into the rental car.

"It's too early for dinner, want to show me Monkesville? Or do you need to get back?"

"We can drive around. Monkesville is a lot like Rocky Point only bigger. I know a place where we can find shaded parking and maybe find some racing going on."

"Racing?"

"My friend Marcie's husband has a set-up here in town for kids to race cars. He's a Grand Prix winner and retired here a little while ago. According to Marcie, teachers love Zack's course because he's really strict about who can drive. Their grades have to be good. Less trouble all around from the teenagers who want to participate."

"Sounds like a great plan. When do they race?"

"I think they practice all the time, then set days for the races, sell tickets, get lots of folks in the stands and make money for maintaining the course. It's fun. I've been a couple of times."

Callie directed him to the old plant with the huge parking lot that had been transformed for racing.

Soon they parked beneath a huge maple nearby, the track clearly visible, but only one car was zooming around.

"Sorry no racing," she said, watching the lone car. "You'll have to use your imagination to see how this works."

"I can do that."

They started back a short time later. Trace studied the different style houses as they headed for the center of town, commenting on the architecture and ornamentation. Some looked almost bleak, weathered wood, no trim. Others had been painted, cared for and dressed up. Gardens abounded everywhere, hollyhocks and gladiolas bobbing in the wind, snapdragons and roses spilling color of every description.

When they reached the main street they decided to get out and walk, window shopping along the way.

At one point Trace guided her around a group of teenagers too busy listening to music and laughing to keep the sidewalk clear.

"They could take that elsewhere," he said.

She nodded. "But they're just kids. If they can't be at the beach, there's not much more for them. I know what it's like. The town in Iowa I grew up in is small with not much to do for farmers' kids."

"Tell me about Iowa," he said as they strolled along.

"Not much to tell. We grow a lot of corn."

"I felt that way about bridge building—the not much to tell part, not the corn part—yet I talked your ear off last night."

"And I enjoyed every moment," she said, surprised to realize how fast the evening had gone.

She glanced at him, startled afresh at how much he looked like Tommy. If she didn't look at him, she could imagine he was someone totally different. But seeing his face, she was instantly reminded of Tommy. And the hurt he'd caused.

Would she ever see Trace without that image?

"So would I like hearing about you," he said. "We were almost related."

She glanced up, caught in his dark gaze. For a long moment Callie felt as if the world was fading. It was hard to breathe, to swallow. That constant flare of attraction startled her and for a shocked moment she wished things had been different—that she'd met Trace first and never known Tommy Warren.

What made her so aware of this man? Was it his looks, so like Tommy's? Trace seemed so different from Tommy. Or was he? She hadn't really known Tommy after all those months, how could she know Trace after two days?

She was jostled by a passerby and quickly stepped aside. She refused to read anything into Trace's comment.

Callie tried to treat their outing like a native showing a visitor around, pointing out the different tourist spots of Monkesville. It worked better if she kept her distance and didn't keep trying to see Tommy in Trace. Her feelings were too confused to make sense. She was angry at Tommy and attracted to his brother.

She led the way purposefully, hoping to outwalk her thoughts.

After Main Street, they wandered through some of the nearby neighborhoods, commenting on houses they liked and the gardens that were flourishing.

Shortly after six, Trace suggested an early dinner.

"It won't take too long to return to Rocky Point. How about we try Sam's Shack for a shrimp dinner?" he said, mentioning a restaurant right on the water in Rocky Point. "I want to be near the sea as much as I can while I'm here," he explained.

"Sounds good."

They returned to the car and began the drive back to

Rocky Point.

Callie hadn't been out to dinner in months except with her friend Margo. No one wanted to invite a grieving woman so soon after her fiancé died.

Another reason to tell the truth. She didn't like getting condolences from people or for some to still assume a solemn expression when near her.

But she didn't want to needlessly hurt the Warrens.

It was too late to announce to the world their breakup without major awkwardness.

Margo knew, but no one else did. She and Callie had been close friends almost since the day Callie moved to Rocky Point.

The restaurant wasn't crowded when they arrived and they were quickly seated at a table by an open window, overlooking the Atlantic with the evening breeze sweeping through.

When their orders had been taken, Trace settled back in his seat and looked at her. "What do you do when you're not working?" he asked. "Hobbies?"

She looked at him warily. "Why?"

He shook his head, his eyes lit in amusement again. "You're cautious and distrustful. I can't help wondering why? Can't I be simply curious?"

She shrugged her shoulders.

"A small business owner seems to be working all the time," she said with a rueful smile. "But when I do break away, I love to swim and sail. I'm part owner in a small sailboat. It's an extravagance, but one I splurged on. Iowa has no sea, obviously, and I love sailing. One of my friends, Margo Benson, got me interested several years ago. We took lessons together right after I moved here and then decided we wanted to keep sailing. So we first bought an old boat, had great fun in that, but moved up a couple of years ago to the one we have now."

"Adventuresome," he murmured. "Did you and Tommy sail together?"

"Of course. We talked about getting a boat of our own once we married. Do you sail?"

"I did a little in college. And when I was working on a project in Indonesia. Haven't been on a boat in ages, unless you count the barges we use to transport materials to the work site up the Amazon."

"That's an amazing river."

"Not fresh and clean like the sea, however. I see the appeal of living in Rocky Point to my parents."

"Yet they rarely go sailing. They're consumed with their art," Callie said. "Tommy hadn't understood that part. He loved the water, loved other activities." Loved almost anything that took him away from painting.

Trace nodded. "We used to vacation on Nantucket Island when we lived in Boston. You couldn't get either of us out of the water unless it was for food."

He fell silent remembering happier days when he and his brother had been close.

Callie wished she'd known both men as boys. Maybe it would have given her some insight into the relationship that seemed doomed to failure from the get go.

While they ate, talk turned to impersonal topics such as books read and movies seen. As far as recent films were concerned, Trace was behind the times because of his work out of the country. But he read a lot. Callie did most of her reading during the winter months. She was taken aback to discover they both enjoyed cozy mysteries. She'd have thought his tastes would run to adventure novels.

"I'd think you'd want to blow off steam after a hard week at work and head for the nearest town to celebrate, not read," she said at one point.

"If you mean take a boat fifty miles down the river to a port town to find a bar for some liquid refreshments, and then try to get transportation back up river in time for work, that's not for me. Some men do it, but drinking in the tropics isn't something I want to do. I'd rather save my time and money for when I can get to a large city, with enough time between jobs to relax, see the sights and maybe restock books. I don't drink much. I won't allow it on the work site. I guess a person gets out of the habit after a while."

Another difference between the brothers.

She had to stop comparing them.

Trace was going to be around for a few days. They'd work together to wind up Tommy's estate and then never see each other again. For a moment she felt dismay. Then shook off the feeling. They had a tenuous connection at best. Do the appraisal, host the retrospective, and then pull back from the Warrens and their family dynamics.

The next afternoon promptly at two, Callie turned into the driveway of Tommy's cottage. She'd done so many times before—the last time being the day she'd surprised him in bed with another woman. Cutting the engine, she sat without moving for a long moment.

Memories assailed. How she'd been so crazy for Tommy's attention she'd rushed here from work many evenings, thrilled to see the man she loved.

At first he'd seemed to be everything she'd want in a husband. But as the weeks slipped by, she realized his lifestyle and values were too different from hers to make a lifelong commitment. Yet she could still remember those heady first days of falling in love.

Sighing for what might have been, she got out of the car and walked to the front door. Knocking, she waited.

Tommy had given her a key, but she didn't feel right using it today. In fact she planned to return the key and her engagement ring to Trace. Tommy had refused the ring that fateful afternoon. He'd begged her to keep it, hoping she'd change her mind. She knew she never would have trusted him again.

She blinked back tears. The shock and devastation of that day swept through her. She wasn't sure she wanted to go inside. It might be better to just back out her car, drive away and come up with some excuse as to why she couldn't do this.

Trace opened the door. He wore worn khaki slacks and a dark blue T-shirt. A blast of cool air swept over her.

"Come in. It's too hot to stand outside," he said, stepping aside and opened the door wider.

"This feels heavenly," she said, stepping into the cottage.

Odd–it looked the same. She'd changed so much since that afternoon, she half expected the cottage to look totally different.

For a moment she expected to see Tommy coming from the back to greet her.

Chapter Seven

Trace closed the door. "Can I get you an iced tea before we tackle the paintings?"

"I'd love some," she said. Anything to delay having to see Tommy's work and be bombarded by the memories they held.

Callie followed Trace into the kitchen. It was spotless.

But empty, no longer Tommy's. No overflowing trash can with beer cans threatening to topple over. No dirty dishes in the sink. No empty pizza boxes stacked on the counter.

"How goes the packing up?" she asked as she waited for the beverage.

"It's going slower than I expected. I've cleared out most of his bedroom and bath. Mom said she'd rented this place furnished, so I don't have to worry about getting rid of furniture. She's still paying rent, but once we're done, she can stop."

"It's hard being here today," Callie said as he handed her a frosty glass of iced tea, keeping one for himself.

"I read the police report. His alcohol level was sky-high. There were maybe a dozen bottles of booze here, most were empty. He had a drinking problem, didn't he? More than just a party guy."

Callie hesitated, taking a sip of the cool beverage, stalling. Finally she nodded. "I think so."

The truth couldn't hurt Tommy any longer.

"I thought he had a problem anyway. We fought several times over it. He said it was just letting off steam. No harm. Ironic, it's what killed him."

Trace nodded as if in confirmation of something he suspected. "He drank in college, as well. I thought he'd cleaned up his act. Guess some things are hard to change. You know where the paintings are?"

"In his studio. I think that's the reason your mother rented this place for him. It has that large lovely room with the bank of windows."

Callie was glad they didn't have to pass the bedroom to reach the studio. It felt strange to be walking around the house knowing Tommy was gone forever.

The studio looked as it had the last time she'd seen it. Tommy had been indifferent much of the time about his body of work, as he called it. Sometimes, like when he was trying hard to get a showing, he'd point out aspects as if she couldn't see them for herself.

Canvasses were stacked all around the room. Some on end, others lying flat. The room was cool and smelled of oil paints and thinner.

"So, do we inventory every one and then you take your time appraising, or work on one at a time?" Trace asked, surveying the chaotic room.

"It's not going to take that long to appraise them," she said. Taking a large tablet from her carryall, she put the bag on the floor and searched for a pen. She also withdrew a small marker pen.

"We'll number the upper left corner of the back of the canvas to keep them straight. We can't call all of them sea view from Rocky Point."

He glanced at the top painting in each stack. They all appeared similar and the description she made would fit each one.

Callie decided to start on the left side of the room and work her way around. She doubted she'd get half done today. But she'd get nothing finished just standing around.

She picked up the first one, marked it with a 1 on the back, and then studied it, turning it to the light.

"So how do you appraise it?" Trace asked, coming to stand beside her.

"For someone who has never sold anything, I would give it what I think its fair market value is." She glanced up at him. "I could be wrong, you know. It could be once these hit the market, people will flock to buy them."

He studied the painting and slowly shook his head. "I don't think so. This one's not all that good. He didn't even cover the canvas here," Trace said, pointing to an area near the left side where the white canvas had been untouched.

She felt awkward about the task ahead. She wanted to be totally honest, her own reputation as an art dealer rested on that.

But she hated letting Tommy's family down. Jocelyn was

going to be so unhappy.

She put the painting down and jotted a note on the pad. Maybe when she totaled it all, it wouldn't seem so bad.

"That's not efficient. It'll take twice as long that way. Let me do the writing, you examine the paintings and dictate what you want to say," Trace said, reaching for the notepad.

His hand almost closed over hers as he took the pad. She felt a flash of awareness at his touch. She almost jumped back.

He looked at the figure noted and then at the painting.

"I think that's generous. My mother's going to be in for a major disappointment. You're right. With what I've seen so far, the ones at your gallery are the best."

"I'm counting on what you said–that your mother's ruthlessly honest about art and doesn't see what's not there because her son did the paintings."

The cooperative effort worked well. Callie spent several minutes on each picture, trying to envision them in appropriate frames, meeting the needs of visitors. She couldn't imagine a collector buying any.

Even allowing for top dollar, she wasn't appraising them very high. And many of the paintings were incomplete--as if Tommy had reached a point where he got bored and moved on to something else. Those were virtually worthless.

Every time she gave an estimate, she glanced at Trace.

He showed no expression, calmly writing down the painting number, a brief description she voiced and the appraised value.

Tommy would have grown bored already and tried to

talk her into something more fun. And she'd likely have given in. He had that way about him.

Trace's stoic manner was starting to make her nervous. She examined another painting. Not all were of seascapes. Tommy had done several canvases of a classic still life. And even a few portraits.

When she came across the nude, she froze. She instantly recognized the woman as the one she'd found with Tommy that fateful afternoon. She couldn't move. Her heart pounded and her hands tightened on the edges of the frame.

She'd forgotten this was here.

She'd gone through all the pictures when Jocelyn insisted on the retrospective. She'd taken the best of the lot. She'd wanted to burn this one, but, of course, had not.

She couldn't bear to look at it.

Trace looked at that picture and then at Callie.

"It's not me," she said.

"I can see that. Some model?"

Callie shrugged, putting the picture down carefully and moving on to the next painting. She attributed no value to it, afraid her voice would betray her if she tried to talk.

The entire process had been going quickly. Now she hoped she would make it through the afternoon.

The light was fading when Callie called a halt. She'd done most of the pictures, only one row remained. Once she had better light, she could quickly appraise them and be done.

She still needed to type up her report. And then present it to Trace for the probate. After a call to Jed to make sure she was in the ball park for an unknown painter of little talent.

"Are these all?" Trace asked.

"As far as I know," Callie said.

She leaned the last picture against the stack, and surveyed how many more remained. "I can finish tomorrow afternoon if you like."

The sooner she finished the better.

"After he left college, Tommy declared he'd become a painter. I'd have expected more from almost twelve years of work. How long does it take to do one painting?"

"It doesn't matter now. He's gone."

Trace looked at her. "I'm sorry. This has to be hard for you."

She shook her head. She didn't want more sympathy. The time for sympathy was when she found out the man she thought she'd marry had cheated on her.

"I need to get going," she said, wanting to flee the memories being here brought.

"Have dinner with me. I'm on leave from work for the first time in five years. I've just lost my brother. My parents are grief-stricken and don't want my company. They say it's too hard looking at me and seeing Tommy. Do you feel that way?"

In his world, no one knew his brother, so no one drew comparisons. But here, he was the outsider, he was the one who looked like the favorite son--but wasn't.

Still, being with Callie brought him closer to Tommy. He hadn't had a chance to say goodbye.

Had his brother known the car was crashing? Had he tried to swerve and avoid the fatal impact?

Trace still couldn't believe he'd died three months ago and he'd only just learned about it. Shouldn't he have felt the world change when Tommy died?

"Okay. I need to change, though. These are old clothes for grubbing around in the studio."

"I'll pick you up in say thirty minutes?" he asked.

He'd ask at the Inn about a nice restaurant. They served meals there, but he wanted to take her somewhere special. Make it a nicer dinner than last night.

"Make it an hour. I'll leave the tablet here. You remember the way to my place?"

He nodded. He'd dropped her off when they'd finished dinner last night. Rocky Point wasn't a very large town, and the streets were neatly laid out in squares.

"I'll find it again."

Once in her car, Callie let the doubts rise. This would be their second dinner together. A second date, virtually.

She wasn't reading more into it than warranted, was she? He was lonely. She could tell him about his brother's last days. He had no idea how hard it was to keep talking about Tommy when she wanted to rail against him for ending things as he had. Still, Trace was family and she knew he needed some closure.

Not that it was her goal in life to comfort Trace Warren. She could think of other things she'd rather do.

Shocked at her wayward thoughts, she started her car and hurried home. She'd be calm, friendly and make sure tonight was the last dinner she shared with him!

He looked too much like Tommy for her. She was getting her emotions mixed up. Just because he looked like Tommy didn't mean he was like him—either in wanting a relationship with her or in being untrustworthy.

Trace was surprised at how much he liked spending time with Callie. Even doing such mundane things as catalog and appraise the oil paintings.

He'd lost his brother even though they hadn't been close. Now was not the time to become interested in anyone. Once things were wrapped up here, he'd be heading back to the Amazon basin and the work that waited.

For the last decade he'd all but severed ties with his family. There was no changing that now, much as he might wish he'd done things differently.

Being with Callie was a link to Tommy.

She was more than a link, however. She intrigued him. He knew she was recovering from the loss of his brother. But it didn't stop him wanting to have her look at him. To see him as a separate man.

He knew he looked like his brother. Would she forever see Tommy each time she looked at him?

Tonight he'd make her see that he was not Tommy.

He was very different, in every way.

He was very much alive. While he hoped to remain that way for a long time, there were no guarantees in life. Building large structures in foreign countries wasn't without risk.

He wondered if that would be his future. He hadn't

questioned his way of life, but Tommy's death had been a wake-up call.

He did want to date, maybe fall a little in love, do things totally different from what he'd been doing since college.

Ever since he'd had to deal with the mess Tommy caused when they'd both been in college, Trace had done his best to avoid his brother and his friends.

Callie was different.

He was tired of playing second fiddle to Tommy. She was someone he could become interested in. Could she ever feel that way about him?

The Pelican Restaurant was just what Trace wanted. Elegant and sophisticated. The linens covering the tables were pristine white and set with heavy silver and crystal goblets. A small dance floor at the far end added an unexpected festive feel to the place, without taking away from the ambiance. Background music played softly until the orchestra came on at nine.

Callie again wore a summery dress. He liked the way she wore feminine clothes—that she didn't mind looking like a woman. He wasn't sure that was her persona for the gallery or her choice for everything. He liked it.

Trace shook his head. He definitely needed a break if he was starting to notice women's clothing.

"Have you eaten here before?" he asked.

"Once or twice," Callie said, perusing the menu. "You may wish to try the sea bass. It's really super. That's what I want."

"Sounds good, but I think I'll have the lobster. Not

something I've had in years," Trace said, ordering for them both a moment later when the waiter appeared to take their choices.

"Did Tommy bring you here?" he asked.

"No. We never came here. This really isn't Tommy's kind of place. Wasn't, I mean."

"What was?"

"Barney's on Atlantic Avenue," she said, naming a nightclub that catered to the younger crowd. "He liked to dance and sing karaoke."

"Tommy sang?"

Trace tried to picture that. He smiled in amusement. He remembered hearing his brother singing in the shower when they were teenagers. He had a terrible voice.

She shook her head, then smiled back. "You don't do that much. Smile, I mean. Tommy was always smiling and laughing. I don't think he took anything seriously."

"Just trying to picture my brother singing in public. Was he any good?"

"Not at all. But after a few beers, he thought he sounded like Elvis," Callie said.

"Do you like Barney's?"

"Occasionally. Not as much as he did. I'm usually tired after working all day. I'm on my feet a lot with the job, both in the gallery and in the framing room, so my favorite spots are quieter. Great, that makes me sound like my grandmother."

"No, I know what you mean. Weekends are fun for going to nightclubs. During the week, a calmer pace is more suitable," Trace said.

She nodded. "Or even staying in."

He glanced at the dance floor, wondering if he should ask her later. He looked at her trying to gauge her reaction to his choice of restaurant. Recommended by the clerk at the Inn, it seemed quite nice to Trace.

"Would you be up to dancing later?" he asked.

"Probably. I love dancing. I don't guess I'd ever be too tired for that."

She smiled again, her gaze drifting around the room.

Trace wondered if he was imagining things, or had she rarely met his eyes since he picked her up?

"Tell me something," he said, waiting for her to look at him.

She did. "What?"

He almost asked what she'd seen in Tommy. But he suddenly didn't want to introduce his brother into every conversation.

"How did an Iowa girl end up in college in Boston?"

"One thing most Iowa farm girls have in common is the desire to leave. Farming is great for my dad. And my mother loves putting up vegetables and fruits. She helps outside, as well. But that wasn't for me. I've always loved art. When one of my grandmothers took me to a gallery in St. Louis one time, I was totally captivated. So combining my desire to leave Iowa behind and study fine paintings and other works, I applied to a school in Boston and one in San Francisco. The one in Boston accepted me first."

"Otherwise you might be in California right now."

"That's right. Maybe. I love the history of this area. Ours in Iowa doesn't go back that far, you know."

"Yet Rocky Point isn't Boston."

"No, I've moved on a bit. But it's still a short hop to get to Boston for a few days away if I want."

"What was the first thing you remember doing when you arrived in Boston?" he asked.

Callie told him about her first year, how she'd played tourist every second she could. The talk veered back toward personal preferences and places they'd both seen. He took a lot of historic locations for granted, having been raised in the old city. She chided him for not appreciating everything more than he did.

Dinner was served and the conversation continued. By the time they'd each had a piece of cheesecake for dessert, Trace felt they'd made strides in forming a friendship of a sort.

It was enough for now.

A small orchestra began to assemble on the dais to the right of the dance floor. In only a few moments the slow rhythm of an old familiar song filled the restaurant.

"Care to dance?" he asked.

"Of course."

She went into his arms as if they'd danced a hundred times before. The floor wasn't crowded, though several other couples joined them. Trace drew her closer, relishing the feel of her against his body. She smelled of some light fragrance, like some elusive flower he couldn't quite name. Her hair was soft against his cheek.

"I love this song," she murmured, leaning back slightly to look up at him.

A spike of awareness hit so hard it stunned him. He wanted this girl who had belonged to his brother. He wanted her more than any other woman he'd ever known.

Without thought, he leaned closer and brushed his lips across hers. For a moment Callie didn't move, then she responded, kissing him back. If they'd been alone, he'd have deepened the kiss. But a modicum of rationality remained— they were in a public place. One, moreover, where Callie was known. Reluctantly he pulled back not wanting to spark any negative gossip she'd have to live with. But the urge to kiss her again burned strongly.

She was breathing hard. So was he for that matter. He stared into her eyes, seeking for some sign she didn't regret the kiss.

She smiled tremulously and rested her forehead against his chin, still dancing.

He wouldn't say a word. What could he say? That he regretted kissing her? That'd be a lie. That he wouldn't do it again? Another lie. If the opportunity arose, he wanted to give her more than a kiss on a dance floor.

Chapter Eight

Callie sat at her desk sipping a latte staring off into space the next morning when Suzanne entered. She closed the door and leaned against it dramatically.

"I just heard. What are you doing?" she asked incredulously.

Callie blinked and looked at her assistant. "Drinking coffee?" she offered, holding up her cup.

"Last night, major clinch scene at the Pelican Restaurant. Half the town knows by now."

"It was just a kiss," Callie defended.

Not true, of course. It could never be classified as *just* anything. It had been amazing. Dreams could be built on such a kiss, if she weren't too levelheaded to know nothing could come of it.

"Did he remind you of Tommy?" Suzanne wanted to know.

"Not at all."

What he reminded her of was the Tommy who might have been. Before her eyes were opened and she discovered him as he truly was. Callie didn't think she could explain that too well. In fact, she couldn't explain any of her feelings clearly. She wasn't sure she could clarify them to herself.

Guilt rose. Should she be kissing anyone so soon after Tommy died? Even though she'd broken their engagement, she'd cared for him. She mourned the loss of the love she'd thought she'd have forever. Was she ready to move on?

She was afraid to find out. What if the next man wasn't for her, either? Would that cause heartache to add to that she already had? A right-thinking person would take time to come to terms with what had happened.

Yet she felt an excitement around Trace she hadn't expected. He made her feel so alive. Last night's kiss had startled her, caught her totally by surprise. And so had the rightness of it.

Or was she confusing him with Tommy?

Lord, don't let me be confusing him with Tommy. Please if this can go anywhere, let me know.

She took another sip of coffee, wishing she wasn't having this conversation with Suzanne. It brought up more questions than she had answers for.

"Are you going to see him again?" Suzanne asked.

Callie nodded. "Of course. I still need to finish the inventory of Tommy's paintings. But that's all—I think."

"So no more dates?"

"Last night wasn't really a date. We merely went to dinner together," Callie tried to explain. She'd thought of it as date.

"After dinner, danced and kissed enough that gossip is running rampant among the locals this morning. I'm sure Jocelyn and Montgomery will hear it before long."

"Oh, no," Callie moaned.

There was always a downside to living in a small community, even one which swelled with tourists in the summer months.

"It was just a kiss, dancing and all. We were caught up in the moment. I know it meant nothing to Trace. Let's forget about it, shall we?"

"If you can. Don't say I didn't warn you if we have a lot of curious browsers today, each wanting to talk to you to see if anything will slip. It'd be so romantic. You lost Tommy, but found his twin. Are they indistinguishable?"

"Good heavens, no. He may look like his twin, but Trace's totally different from Tommy."

Was she getting the two of them confused? Was she trying to find a connection to replace the one severed by Tommy's betrayal?

No. She knew the difference. The brothers were not interchangeable.

Trace was a hard worker. He had already risen fairly high in the construction world to be in charge of such mammoth building sites like the one in the Amazon. His superiors depended upon him, as did all the men and women who worked for him.

Was he the kind of person who would cheat on anyone? She didn't know him that well, but something told her Trace Warren would never do such a thing to someone he professed to care for.

"Well, it could be romantic," Suzanne said with a smile on her face.

"Suzanne, I have no interest in Trace Warren beyond working with him to wind up Tommy's estate. If anyone really needs to see me, do come get me. But you handle any gawkers."

"Sure thing, boss." She laughed softly and slipped back into the gallery.

Callie shook her head. She so did not need further complications in her life.

Please, Lord, a quiet day would be wonderful.

She finished the tax forms she was working on and cleared her desk so she could move to the framing room. She enjoyed the variety of tasks needed to run a successful gallery.

No sooner had she begun to frame a new acquisition than Suzanne popped her head in, holding Callie's cell phone.

"Jocelyn Warren calling," she said.

Callie sighed and put down the frame. "Thanks," she said, reaching for the phone.

"Good morning, Jocelyn, what can I do for you?" she said in her very best professional voice as if that'd have any effect on Jocelyn.

"I've heard a disturbing rumor and you can set the record straight," Jocelyn said without preamble. "You and Trace dined out last night and were kissing and dancing for hours. I can't believe the rumors people spread. How preposterous."

"Which part?" Callie asked carefully. She did not need Jocelyn's interference.

"That you'd be dating so soon after Tommy died for one thing. And to go out with Trace would be beyond anything. He's Tommy's brother. He should have more sense."

"We went out for dinner, Jocelyn. He kindly offered to buy me a meal after we worked on appraising Tommy's paintings yesterday afternoon."

"At the Pelican?" She sounded horrified.

"Why not? It's a nice place. It was recommended so he took me there."

"Dancing? Kissing?" Her voice rose several levels.

"We danced a couple of times after our meal. Maybe there was a brushing of lips," Callie said, trying to minimize things. It wasn't as if she owed Jocelyn any explanation. But she felt compelled to respond though she didn't need to justify herself to Tommy's mother. How would Jocelyn feel if she knew the truth about Tommy?

"Callie, do you think that's wise? You had a terrible shock when Tommy died. I know Trace looks like him, but he's not Tommy. I know you loved my son. We all did. Don't confuse them."

Callie knew it was the grieving mother speaking, but she was suddenly defensive and annoyed that Jocelyn thought she had the right to talk to her this way. She'd tried to protect Tommy's memory by not mentioning that last afternoon to his parents.

Maybe that'd been a mistake.

"I am not confusing them. Trace likes to talk about Tommy. They were twins, close at one time, he says. Over the last few years other commitments kept them apart. I think he enjoys hearing what I can tell him about Tommy."

In fact, that could be the only reason he spent time with her.

The thought made her vaguely depressed.

There was silence for a moment. Then Jocelyn spoke in a strained voice. "It's just so soon after Tommy died. I'd think his memory deserved more respect."

"His memory deserves all the respect we can give it," Callie said gently. "Trace and I are not doing anything to disrespect that. Trace is your son, too. He grieves for Tommy's death."

"I miss him so much," Jocelyn said before Callie could say any more. "He was the sweetest little boy. Always so affectionate. And talented. I can't bear to think of his being gone forever."

"Trace's being home must bring you some comfort," Callie said.

She didn't understand the Warrens. If she'd had a family member die, she'd want the rest of the family close by to offer comfort and to remember together.

"Trace never understood his brother."

Or maybe he understood him all too well, Callie thought with sudden insight.

"I should have known that you were not dating again. Now that you said it was a working dinner I understand better. But kissing Trace. My dear, I know he looks like Tommy, but I don't think that's wise."

"I didn't kiss him because he looks like Tommy."

What a horrible thought. Surely Trace didn't believe that.

"Put it down to the mood of the evening. Jocelyn, we all miss Tommy."

"I know. And I for one shall miss him all my life. In time you'll move on. I know that, but not yet. It's too soon."

Callie made a noncommittal sound.

"How is the appraisal coming?" Jocelyn asked in a bracing voice.

"I was able to complete more than half yesterday afternoon," Callie said, glad for the change of topic.

"Half. Good heavens, are you spending enough time on each one? That seems quite fast to me."

"There aren't that many canvases. I'd say we did about eighty yesterday. I'm more than half through."

"You must be mistaken. Tommy painted for years. Even given he was slow when starting there should be hundreds of paintings."

"There aren't at the cottage. Would he have some elsewhere?"

"I don't understand. There should be years worth of work," Jocelyn repeated.

Callie had thought so herself before she suspected Tommy's method was to paint when there was nothing else to do.

"Maybe he was a perfectionist and destroyed work he didn't consider good enough to keep," Callie suggested. She knew some painters did that.

"I'll have to talk with Montgomery. Trace is being quite unreasonable about following the terms of the will."

"His responsibility is to do so," Callie defended.

Why wouldn't he? Sometimes she wondered about Jocelyn's grasp of reality.

"We'll see how the showing goes," Jocelyn said. "He's sure to see his brother in a different light after the opening."

When Callie ended the call, she wondered yet again if she should have told Jocelyn and Montgomery everything about their relationship. And the truth of the paintings.

By late afternoon she had accomplished a great deal in framing the paintings she planned for Tommy's show. She was tired, but in a pleasant way.

Suzanne had been spot-on with her predictions of more visitors to the gallery. She'd fielded the curiosity. Sales had been up and interest was growing about the retrospective of Tommy's work. Callie hoped pent-up curiosity would make it a stellar show for Jocelyn's and Montgomery's sake. The family was well known in Rocky Point and surroundings. She hoped people would flock to see what Jocelyn's son had produced.

She locked up at six and headed for home. Unless the weather was too awful, she normally walked the few blocks. Reaching her flat, she quickly changed and then went to the kitchen to see what she could throw together for dinner.

There was a knock at the door.

When she opened it, Trace stood there, dressed casually, large pizza box in hand.

"Dinner?" he asked.

A spurt of joy went through her. She studied him for a long moment, wondering why he'd come.

"Your timing's perfect. I was just gazing at all the things

in the refrigerator wondering what would miraculously fix itself. I love pizza. But I'm a bit surprised to see you."

"I called my folks, but Dad was in the studio and didn't plan to stop for something as mundane as dinner. Mom was lying down. She said she has a headache. I could tell by her voice she was feeling tired. So rather than eat alone in the dining room at the Inn, I took the chance you'd be free."

She stepped aside and motioned for him to enter.

He glanced around her apartment and then looked at her, raising an eyebrow. "Where do we eat?"

"Since the balcony's too tiny for both of us, it'll have to be the dining table. I'll clear it off."

It was cluttered with mail and magazines. She swept them into a pile and put it all on her coffee table. A quick scan of the room showed the rest was in passable condition for drop-in company.

Had she known anyone was coming, she'd have made sure the place was spotless.

"Have a seat and I'll get plates, napkins and something to drink. I have wine, beer or soft drinks."

"I'll have a cola if you have it," he said, putting the large box in the center of the table.

Callie got the items needed and returned in only moments.

She wasn't sure how to take Trace's unexpected arrival.

And she was disturbed by the burst of joy she experienced when she opened the door. She was trying to keep this relationship on an even, business-like keel.

She didn't have a single other business relation where the

person showed up on her doorstep with pizza.

But his explanation sounded genuine. She knew he didn't know many people in Rocky Point.

When she returned, he stood near the short hallway that led to her bedroom, studying one of the oil paintings on the wall.

"This isn't Tommy's," he commented.

The half falling-down, weathered wooden barn stood on a lonely expanse of prairie. The painting captured the feeling of desolation and lost hopes.

"No."

She pointed to a black-and-white pen drawing framed and hanging near the front door.

"That one is, however. He gave me that on one of our first dates."

The drawing was of an overturned rowboat, paddles nearby. Small, only about six inches square, it was a excellent pen-and-ink drawing.

"So who did the barn?" he asked, looking back to that one.

"I did."

Trace looked surprised. "I didn't know you painted."

"I don't do much anymore. I'm not that good. I love being around excellent works of art, so running the gallery suits me better. So does the more regular income."

"You are good. That painting evokes a myriad of feelings. Has my mother seen your work?" Trace asked. "Do you have others?"

"I painted when I was younger. There're a couple in my

bedroom. Mostly from Iowa, so they remind me of home."

"Nothing here sparks your imagination?"

"Sometimes. Mostly I focus on the gallery and what I can offer customers."

Callie was secretly pleased he liked the painting she'd done when feeling homesick her first few months in Boston. Not that she'd kid herself she had any future in painting, but it was nice to have someone say something nice about the scene.

"So what did you do all day?" she asked when they sat at the table.

She was curious to learn what he'd find to do in Rocky Point. He must be champing at the bit to return to building that bridge.

"More of the same–packed up the rest of Tommy's things. I called a dealer to look at the few pieces of furniture that were his. They're not worth much. Nothing old enough to be an antique. Nothing new enough to command top dollar. Except for the paintings, the place is ready to turn back to the owner."

They each served themselves. She filled two glasses with ice and cola and sat back to enjoy the pizza. The topping had everything but anchovies. The best kind, she thought taking the first bite.

"So you'll be leaving now?" she asked. Disappointment flared.

"I'm not sure. A couple of days ago I'd have said yes. Now, I may hang around a little longer. If Mom can get beyond seeing Tommy when she looks at me, I'd like to spend a bit more time with my parents. It might be years before I can make it back."

"Stay for the retrospective. I think your parents would be glad of your support for that."

"Dad came by the cottage to see me today."

Trace took another slice of pizza and put it on his plate. He looked at Callie, his gaze catching hers.

"He's in the midst of a new sculpture. His way of dealing with grief, lose himself in his work. We don't seem to have much to talk about."

"So why did he come?"

"Apparently he heard about our dinner last night."

Callie suspected where this was going. "And?"

"I know you're grieving for my brother. Was last night about Tommy?"

"No."

She couldn't say much more because she wasn't sure what last night had been about.

She didn't want Trace to think he was a substitute for his brother–not with her or with his parents.

She looked at the pizza.

"Was that the reason for pizza, so we wouldn't be seen in public?"

Trace laughed aloud. "Nothing so ulterior. I like pizza and took a chance you would as well. They don't have delivery in the Amazon."

"I should tell you it was a great day at the gallery because of everyone dropping by to glean what they could. Fortunately for me, Suzanne was there to field the inquiries."

"I've never lived in a small town before. Sounds like something I wouldn't like," Trace said.

"It'll pass. Your being here is news. Your family's well-known and I think everyone's fascinated to see Tommy's image walking around."

"We may look alike, but we're not at all alike," he repeated.

"I've figured that out myself," Callie said.

"I'm not out to antagonize my parents. They have enough to deal with. I wouldn't mind seeing your boat, however."

"That can be arranged. We could even take a quick sail today if you like. It'll be light for a couple of more hours," she said.

Chapter Nine

Truth be told, she'd like to get out of the intimacy of dining together in her apartment. She found herself studying him as he ate, noting how his hair was cut, wondering if it felt as thick as his brother's.

It was hard to look at him and not see Tommy, but gradually she was seeing Trace's personality stamped on his features. His own quiet ways, different from the flamboyance she'd dealt with before. She wasn't sure how she felt about it. It was so strange to see Tommy's features and hear different thoughts come from that mouth.

She gave Margo a call when they finished eating to make sure she didn't have plans for the boat.

"Not this week. Maybe I'll want to take it out next weekend. I was going to call you to see if you wanted to do an overnight up the coast."

"I'll see. I want to show it to a friend tonight."

"The same friend you were kissing last night at the Pelican?" she teased.

"Good grief, the rumor mill has been working if you heard it at work." Margo worked as a nurse at the hospital in Monkesville.

"Which does not answer my question."

"Yes, I'm taking Trace to see the boat. Satisfied?"

"Might be. He anything like his brother?"

"No."

"Good. Have fun."

Callie started to tell Margo it was only a kind gesture to a visitor, but conscious of Trace standing nearby, she refrained. "Thanks. Call me next week and we can discuss a trip."

She ended the call and turned.

"We're all set. She doesn't have plans," she said, feeling a sudden awareness that had her heart pounding. Wiping her palms on her shorts, she stepped back.

Was it her imagination or did Trace seem to take up more room in her apartment than other visitors?

The remaining pizza was wrapped and put in the refrigerator, the glasses in the sink, trash disposed of and they were off.

Walking down to the harbor, Callie was conscious of the curious glances they received. She wondered what comments would circulate tomorrow. The sooner they were on the boat, the better as far as she was concerned.

"This is it," she said with some pride when they reached the slip. It was an eighteen-foot, single-masted boat, bobbing quietly in the slip.

The water was slightly choppy from the westerly wind. The sun was in the west, but would not set for another couple of hours.

"She's a beauty," Trace said.

"Margo and I think so. Come aboard."

Callie stepped onboard and did a quick inspection, starting the blower to clear any gas fumes. When they were ready to leave, she looked at him.

"Can you swim? I have life jackets that I insist people wear if they can't swim."

"I can swim," Trace said.

"Okay, then. The jackets are in that compartment. I take a couple out to have on deck and readily available in case of an emergency. Not that we've had one yet. I want to be prepared."

She competently backed out of the slip using the single engine. Carefully keeping below the speed limit, she cleared the harbor.

"Good wind tonight," she said, cutting the engine and beginning to raise the sail.

"Can I help?" Trace asked.

"Sure, pull this line until the sail is fully extended."

The boat quivered a moment as the sail flapped in the wind. Once the line was secure, she spun around and set the tiller to take advantage of the wind. The boat seemed to leap forward skimming the water as if in a race.

Trace sat beside her on the narrow bench seat. Land fell behind them as they moved out into the bay.

"Isn't this great?" Callie asked.

She raised her face to the sky, enjoying the freedom of the boat. Turning to Trace, she smiled broadly. "If I could, I'd sail every day. I'm so glad you brought dinner so I could thank you this way."

"Me, too." He leaned forward to kiss her.

Callie didn't know what to do–let go of the tiller and throw her arms around Trace or pull back and try to keep her distance.

While she was deciding, Trace's kiss sparked an answering response deep within. She turned slightly for a better connection. This was as close to heaven as she'd yet reached–sailing while kissing such an exciting man.

The boat waffled. She broke the kiss and trimmed the sail, turning into the wind again.

"I need to concentrate," she said, feeling flustered.

"Wouldn't want you to capsize us," Trace said with a grin.

"It's a reliable boat. We'll be fine. But I do need to pay attention."

Trace settled back to enjoy the ride.

Callie's heart pounded. She'd thought sailing would be a better idea than staying in her apartment. Now she wasn't so sure. They were of necessity sitting close due to the size of the seat.

And if he kissed her again, she didn't think she'd put up much resistance.

Maybe this had been a bad idea.

But Trace made no move to kiss her again. She sailed outbound for about a half hour, then turned to head back. It would take longer to return tacking against the wind.

Once the tension eased from the kiss, she enjoyed the sail. It was just what she needed to keep things in perspective. Trace was leaving soon. There was nothing between them. Any feelings she thought she felt were probably because he looked so much like Tommy.

"Can you come tomorrow to finish the appraisals?" he asked at one point.

"Saturdays are our busiest day. We have all the weekenders in town, as well as the summer residents coming and going. And some locals actually shop at the gallery, as well. With the publicity I'm starting to generate for the retrospective, I'm hoping more locals will stop in."

"When then?"

"Sunday afternoon?"

"Not Sunday morning?" he asked.

"I'll be at church in the morning."

"Which one?"

"Trinity. Do you know it?"

He nodded. "The few times I went to a church when my folks first moved here, I attended Trinity. Did Tommy attend with you?"

She shook her head. "No, he usually went out until late on Saturday nights and so slept in on Sundays."

It had been a bone of contention between them in the early days. After a while, Callie had stopped asking him to join her.

Another area in which they didn't agree.

"Do you want to come with me?" she asked.

"I'd like that. What time?"

"Eleven. I'll meet you out front." The moment she issued the invitation she wondered if that'd been wise.

To have Trace accept and plan to attend with her

startled her.

"We have services Sunday mornings at the build site, an old catholic priest makes the trek up the river faithfully every week for those who wish to attend," Trace said. "That's dedication. He comes even in the rain, fog, or blazing sun."

"To share the Lord," she murmured. "Do many of the workers go to see him?"

"Most, actually."

"Including you?"

"Including me."

This was a different side of Trace she hadn't expected. Tommy had been adamant that Sunday mornings were for sleeping in. She'd tried so hard at first to get him to come with her to hear the message, but never succeeded.

"Maybe we can have lunch after church and then get to the appraisals," he suggested.

She nodded, her heart rate bumping up again. "I'd like that. If we eat at Marcie's I can get her to hold us a table. Her place really fills up fast on Sundays in the summer."

"It's a date."

She caught her breath. It shouldn't be a date. She knew gossip would be rampant.

But she didn't care. For once she wanted to do what felt right, even if it did cause tongues to wag.

She could easily finish the appraisals Sunday afternoon. Then she really had no further tie with Trace.

Unless she could get him interested in the retrospective and stay until it was over.

She was really reaching now. Hadn't the showing already

been a bone of contention between him and his parents? Would he change his mind now and stay if she asked him to?

When they reached the harbor, they dropped the sail, furled it, then headed in under power.

"Thank you, Callie," Trace said formally when they were tied up. "It's much more refreshing to sail the bay than up the Amazon."

He offered his hand to help her to the dock. She took it, feeling the hard calluses from work. He was slow to release hers.

"Anytime," she said with a smile. It had been a refreshing ending to the evening.

Would they ever go out again? For a longer sail than just a quick run after dinner?

She doubted it. Not unless she sailed to South America and up that river.

She nodded to a couple who moored their boat two slips down as they passed on the dock. She wondered if she'd hear about this tomorrow. Didn't anyone have better things to do than speculate on her love life?

Hardly that. She wasn't in love with Trace. Not sure she was even in like. Though those kisses gave her some pause.

They walked back to her flat in the growing twilight. The summer evenings were warm enough to enjoy, cool enough to be pleasant without the heat of the day. Families were out on Harbor Street, enjoying the outdoor dining or strolling along with treats from the ice-cream parlor. Children ran and dodged in and out among the other pedestrians. Groups of teenagers hung out with music blaring from their ear buds.

"We don't sit outside much in the evening because of the insects," Trace said. "We have modified tents, with elevated wooden floors and canvas sides that can be rolled up for whatever breeze is passing through. Radio reception is rare."

"So mostly you read," she said, remembering what he said at dinner the other evening.

"That and woodworking. I make toys and furniture for the children of my local workers. They don't have much as a rule and it keeps me busy."

She looked at him. "Then you are an artist. I'd love to see some of your work. Do your parents know?"

"Woodworking as a hobby is not the same thing as being an artist," he repeated carefully.

"Counts in my book. What kind of toys?"

He described some of the pull toys for toddlers, the cradles and high chairs for both dolls and children.

"The best thing is the wood is so available. What we cut, we use," he finished.

"Do you have any pictures of your work?"

"It's not art, Callie, just toys for kids."

"I wasn't thinking of representing it, I'm curious."

When they reached her apartment building, she invited him in.

"Not tonight, but I'll walk you up," Trace said.

When they reached her door, he leaned an arm against the jamb, looking at her.

"Thank you, Callie, for taking me out in your boat."

"I'm glad you came," she said, wondering if he'd kiss her

once more.

He did–slowly reaching out for her and pulling her close. His kisses were special, no denying that.

She looped her arms around his neck and gave herself up to pure enjoyment. It'd been far too long since she'd been kissed like this. Like she was the most important thing in the world. She felt young, alive and feminine. She wanted more than kisses. She wanted the promise of love that had been hers for such a short time. The expectation of being a couple that would surpass her dreams.

As Trace's mouth left hers to trail kisses against her cheek, along her jaw, at that pulse point in her throat, she felt as if she were floating. It had been too long.

"Tommy," she murmured.

Chapter Ten

Trace reared back as if slapped. For a moment he couldn't believe what he heard. She thought he was Tommy. Or was using him as some kind of substitute for his dead brother.

Callie opened her eyes, gazing up at him in horror. "Trace."

He pulled her arms down and stepped back.

"I'm sorry," she said.

"Yeah, well, I should have expected it, shouldn't I? It's too soon since his death for you to move on. I'm not a substitute, though, Callie."

He turned and walked away.

"Wait, please," she called after him.

He kept walking.

It wasn't the first time he'd been mistaken for Tommy. When they'd been kids, Tommy had often told people he was Trace to create mischief.

Trace hadn't liked it then, he didn't like it now. He was fooling himself that anything could develop between him and Callie. She'd forever see Tommy. It was good he found out. Saved wear and tear on the heart later.

He got into the rental car and returned to the Inn. He'd asked earlier to have his room changed if one with a sea view became available.

He no longer planned to stay that long. Tomorrow he'd see what steps he could take to wind up the estate with or without his being present.

With the rest of his leave, he'd visit some friends in Boston or find a cool mountain to visit for a complete change from the Amazonian jungle.

The message light was flashing on his phone when he entered his room. Suspecting it was Callie with some apology, he ignored it. He poured himself a drink from the in-room bar and sat in the sole chair, gazing out the darkened window at the few lights he could see. Keeping his thoughts at bay, he ignored the anger that hovered at the thought of Callie's confusing the two of them.

He'd known her less than a week. There was no deep emotional attachment.

He was confusing her kindness to Tommy's brother with a genuine interest in himself.

She hadn't led him on. If anything, she'd been shy and hesitant. He was pushing. And he wasn't sure why.

Was it merely a flare of attraction stronger than anything he'd felt before?

There was no future for them even if she saw him apart from Tommy. He was committed to finishing that bridge and when it was complete, there were others to build. She lived in this vacation resort town, had built her business here and it wasn't portable enough to take anywhere.

He frowned. Why was he thinking of a future, anticipating roadblocks where none would be needed. He was not falling for the woman who loved his brother.

He took another sip of his drink then decided to call it a night. The phone rang again. Trace glanced over his shoulder, but made no move to answer it. There was nothing to say.

Callie let the phone ring until it switched to the automatic message recording. She hung up. She'd already left a message. Leaving dozens wouldn't help if Trace refused to answer the phone or return her call.

She leaned her head back against the chair, anger at her stupidity flooding.

How could she have said such a thing? She hadn't been thinking of Tommy, except to mourn the loss of the love she thought would be with her forever.

She'd been kissing Trace. She knew that. Why had Tommy's name slipped out?

Maybe because Trace's kisses were much more affecting than Tommy's had been. She'd been questioning the difference. That excuse sounded dumb to her own ears.

Picking up her phone again she dialed her friend's number.

Margo answered after three rings.

"Were you asleep?" Callie asked.

"Of course, it's almost midnight and I have to get to work tomorrow. What's up?"

"I made a colossal mistake tonight."

"Doing?"

Callie hesitated. She wanted her friend's advice. But she felt like an idiot admitting to what she'd done.

"When Trace kissed me I said Tommy's name," she said in a rush.

There was silence on the line for a moment. Then, "Let me get this straight, you're lip-locked with the brother of your dead fiancé and when you come up for air you call Tommy's name?"

"Not really. I mean, yes, that's what it looks like, but I wasn't really calling Tommy."

"The kiss reminded you of Tommy?"

"Not at all."

"Better or worse?" Margo asked.

"Much better."

"So maybe you had better stick to some pet name and leave first names behind. What were you thinking?"

"I wasn't. I don't know why I said Tommy's name. But Trace thinks I was using him as a substitute for his brother. He left angry. I don't blame him. I tried calling, but he's not answering. I left a message, but he hasn't called back."

"I'm not surprised. Think about it a minute, Callie. What if he'd been kissing you like there's no tomorrow and then murmurs another woman's name in your ear?"

"I would hate it," she said, depressed.

"Probably made worse because of the twin thing," Margo added. "No one knows Trace around here. Everyone knew Tommy. He's probably had to fend off comments his entire stay. Girlfriend, you need to do some major apologizing."

"I tried. He wouldn't listen before he left. Now he won't call me back. Don't just tell me what I should do, I already know. Give me some hints on how to do it."

Margo gave the matter some thought.

"If it were me, I'd get up early, get some luscious breakfast from Marcie's place and surprise him in the morning."

"And if he won't open the door?"

"At least you'd have a great breakfast."

"I don't know."

"Hey, nothing ventured, nothing gained. Besides, you'll catch him off guard with early breakfast and get to see what he looks like first thing in the morning. Not all bad."

Callie laughed. "I'm sure he'll care less about making a good impression. He probably hates me."

"More likely he's hurt you'd confuse them," Margo said seriously.

"I didn't confuse them. Not really." Callie thought about it for a minute. "Maybe I should tell him the truth about Tommy."

"My guess is it wouldn't come as a huge surprise to Trace," Margo said dryly.

"Um, maybe. It would to his mother, I think. That's why I didn't say anything. I didn't want to tarnish her memories of her son."

"You can't keep protecting Jocelyn Warren your whole life. She's a grown-up. It's her son. Let her deal with things the way they are, not the way she wants them to be."

"Oh, Margo, she lost him. She doted on him and he

died. She'll never get over it. The least I can do is help ease the pain during this transition time."

"You're too nice, Callie. You don't really think this showing of Tommy's paintings is going to do any good, do you?"

"Sometimes I feel I let him down. In retrospect, I should have given him a show."

"At the time you had to think of the gallery's reputation. This retrospective will be a nice tribute, everyone will feel good, but no one's going to buy those paintings."

"Maybe not. But putting on the show will help Jocelyn and Montgomery, I know it. I can't imagine the pain of losing a child. I'm still sad he died and I was so angry at him that last day I can't stand it. How much worse for a mother to lose a cherished son?"

"That's a reason I can understand. Go to bed. Get up early and woo the brother."

Callie laughed and bid her friend good-night. She didn't want to woo Trace.

Or did she?

Callie hadn't needed Margo's example to make her feel bad. She knew Trace thought she was dreaming of Tommy. If he only knew the truth would it change things? Probably not.

She was too wary of getting involved again with another man—especially one who looked exactly like Tommy.

She'd lived with the cover-up for all these months, she wouldn't tell him now. It didn't matter. And her reasons stood, she didn't want to cause Jocelyn any more grief.

She set her alarm early, wondering if she could go through with Margo's idea.

It was not yet seven when Callie knocked on the door to Trace's room. Fortunately she knew the owner of the Inn and had told Shannon that she was delivering something for Tommy's brother. The magic words.

Callie still felt guilty when people were so solicitous about her loss. If they only knew.

The large basket Marcie had provided was heavy. Callie hoped she didn't have to turn and leave without Trace even being tempted.

The door swung opened abruptly.

"That didn't take long," Trace said. He was wearing a towel wrapped around his waist and drying his hair with another. He stopped abruptly when he saw Callie.

"I thought you were room service," he said, looking at the festive basket in her hands.

"Sort of." She held up the basket. "Breakfast is served."

She held her breath, hoping he wouldn't slam the door in her face.

"This is what the Inn serves up now?"

"No, this is what I serve. May I?"

She could hardly keep her gaze from his broad chest. The skin was bronze and taut over his muscular chest. There were more differences between him and Tommy than he knew. She swallowed hard. So much tantalizing skin so early in the morning wasn't good for her equilibrium.

He stepped to one side and opened the door wide.

She walked in and over to the small table beneath the

window. There was only one chair. One of them would have to sit on the rumpled bed. She looked away. That would not be her!

Try to focus, she admonished herself as she placed the basket in the center and began to withdraw the china and silverware Marcie had insisted upon when she learned of Callie's mission. She'd been delighted with the idea of the early morning breakfast surprise and surpassed herself.

"I have eggs Benedict, some homemade cinnamon rolls and a fruit compote," she said as she withdrew the warming trays from the wicker. "And coffee, of course."

Trace had not yet said a word. Glancing over her shoulder, she met his eyes.

"What's this for?" he asked guardedly.

"To make amends. I need to go on record I was not thinking of Tommy when his name slipped out. I was fully involved in the kiss you and I were sharing."

It sounded lame when she said it aloud. She'd rehearsed it all the way over. Darn it, would he believe her?

"No amends needed. It's not a big deal."

He shrugged and headed for the bathroom. "I'll get dressed and join you."

That'd give her a few moments to get some control of her emotions, Callie hoped. They ranged from hopeful to discouraged. His comment hadn't been very encouraging. And she suspected it had been a bigger deal to Trace than he was willing to admit.

She had everything set when he came back into the bedroom. She'd opened the window to let some of the fresh air blow in before the heat of the day made it uncomfortable. She'd also debated making the bed, but that might have been a bit too presumptuous.

Trace sat on the edge of the bed and called to cancel the breakfast he'd ordered. Then he drew the table closer, looking at the elaborate feast.

"This is nicer than anything I've had in a long time," he said sincerely. He met her glance and inclined his head slightly. "Thanks."

"My pleasure."

She waited for him to begin to eat before starting herself. The hot food had retained the heat in the warming tray. The fruit was icy cold. She was pleased with the way things had turned out. Now if this only mended fences.

"Are you still coming to church tomorrow morning?" she asked once they'd begun to eat.

He looked thoughtful for a moment, then shrugged. "I might as well."

As an answer, it wasn't overwhelmingly positive, but she felt encouraged by his response. At least he hadn't said no.

As the silence began to stretch out, Callie hoped Trace would initiate a conversation. She was afraid to say anything less the tenuous truce be broken. She didn't want to talk about Tommy or his paintings or their parents.

It left little to talk about, she realized with depressing recognition. Anything personal would be viewed as suspect. They'd discussed other topics at their other meals, why couldn't she think up something now?

The room phone rang. Callie gave a brief sigh of thanks.

At least the growing awkwardness would dissipate while he spoke on the phone.

It was his mother. She obviously asked what he was doing because he said calmly eating breakfast with Callie.

Without any more explanation, did Jocelyn think she'd stayed the night and now they were sharing breakfast? Callie was horrified. She shook her head frantically at Trace.

"What?" he asked, covering the mouthpiece.

"Make sure your mother knows I just brought it by," she hissed.

Amusement danced in his eyes as he realized why she was telling him that. Without agreeing, he removed his hand.

"Mother, Callie and I are adults. I'm sure what we do in our free time is our own concern."

Callie gave a small groan. She could imagine what Jocelyn was thinking!

"Now why would I want to do that?" he asked. He listened another moment then spoke again, "I'm not sure I'm staying for long."

Obviously Jocelyn had a lot to say. Trace was silent for several moments, his eyes steady on Callie. She began to fidget. Eating was impossible.

"I'll come by this afternoon, then," he said.

When he replaced the phone, he returned to the table.

"So what did your mother say?" she asked.

"She seemed startled to learn you were here."

"I'm not surprised the way you made it sound. You should have told her I brought breakfast early."

"Then she'd want to know why."

"Oh, like thinking I stayed the night is preferable to that?"

"We're both adults," he began.

"Maybe, but I'm not having my reputation dragged through the gossip mill to give you some kind of amusing way to string your mother along. She must be horrified."

"Are you supposed to forego dating because Tommy died?" he asked. "It's been several months."

"We're not dating. But I bet your mother thinks so, doesn't she? You should have told her the truth."

"She didn't call about that. She asked me to stay at the cottage while I'm here," he said.

Callie put down her fork. "You've been here several days. Why move to the cottage now?"

"Apparently she's worried someone will break in to steal the paintings. I'm to be the guard."

Callie looked at him. She could tell he was amused. "Are you serious?"

"Don't you think it ironic? Mom couldn't wait for me to be gone since I'm not fawning over the paintings like she is, yet someone must have suggested the possibility of some summer visitors helping themselves to the inventory. She thinks they'd make a killing. We need to complete the appraisals and get a monetary amount set for probate," he said. "And somehow, my mother needs to see Tommy's paintings."

Back to business. At least he was talking again.

"So are you moving into the cottage to guard the paintings?" she asked.

"I haven't decided. I thought to head out pretty soon."

Probably because there was nothing around town for him to stay for.

"I'd love you to stay for the exhibit," she said again.

"Why?"

"To see it, of course. It might be the only showing of your brother's work."

He rubbed his cheek and chin. He had not had time to shave and the rasping noise could clearly be heard. Callie watched him warily.

"We'll see," he said at last.

It wasn't until they were sipping the last of the fragrant coffee that Callie began to relax and believe maybe Trace had accepted her apology. Not that he'd said anything to that end. If anything he'd remained a bit distant. But she deserved that for her faux pas. She hoped they could recapture the camaraderie she thought was developing between them.

"If I move my stuff to the cottage, I'll let you know. At least the cottage has a view of the sea. What's the point of staying on Rocky Point if all I'm looking at is trees?" he said.

She wasn't sure she liked the idea of him staying at the cottage. Visiting there would forever remind her of the day she found her fiancé in bed with another woman. But she dare not tell Trace. Not and keep Tommy's memory intact for his family.

When he put his cup down, she began to gather all the used dishes and utensils to return to Marcie. The basket was soon packed and she had no reason to linger.

"I'll see you a bit before eleven at Trinity tomorrow,"

she said, carrying the now lighter basket to the door.

He studied her for a moment then nodded.

"Thank you for breakfast. Apology accepted. But last night was an epiphany. You aren't over Tommy and I'm not ready for any kind of relationship. I have my work waiting and a long-distance affair can't last. Things happen for a reason and I think last night was a clear warning. Let's keep our interaction on a business basis, shall we?"

"Of course." Callie kept the stupid smile plastered on her face until the door closed behind her. Then let it slip. Maybe breakfast had mended fences, but not entirely the way she wanted.

Chapter Eleven

By two o'clock Sunday afternoon when Callie arrived at the cottage, she'd decided to adhere to Trace's request to keep things purely business.

There had been some awkwardness at church that morning. Several friends had joined her and been introduced to Trace. Afterward, he'd said nothing about lunch together, so they'd parted ways.

Again she berated herself for the stupid mistake of Friday night.

She wasn't certain in her own mind if she was attracted to Trace or to the illusion that Tommy once offered. Was she looking for some kind of relationship that would give her everything she expected and not be one full of pitfalls and reality?

"Show me where you would have me go, Lord. Let me be content with all I now have." she murmured as she made her way up the short walkway to the cottage door.

Was she ready to trust another man with her heart? She didn't think so. Margo was the one always surging ahead, certain the current man she was dating was Mr. Right. Callie was more conservative.

And after Tommy's actions, doubly wary of trusting.

She was determined to finish the work this afternoon and be out of Trace's way.

Trace met her at the door.

Callie greeted him calmly, belying the rapid increase in her heart rate. Without looking directly at him, she went straight to the studio. It was the same as they'd left it a few days ago.

"We'll do it that same way as before?" he asked, picking up the clipboard.

"Sure."

She picked up the first picture, wishing she could rush through the job and get out. But she owed it to Tommy and her own sense of artistic integrity to do the best job she could.

Jotting a number on the back, she studied the scene for a moment then began her assessment.

It grew easier as they progressed. There wasn't much difference in either the style, execution or composition of the paintings. It was as if Tommy found one scene he liked and replicated it whenever he felt like painting. She couldn't even tell how recently he painted the scenes.

The afternoon was growing late by the time the last canvas was valued. Callie set it back against the stack she'd been working on and looked at Trace.

"It'll take me a few days to get everything put into a format you can use for tax purposes. This is my professional opinion of the paintings worth. You may receive more or less upon sale."

"Understood," Trace said.

"You may wish to ask another appraiser for his or her valuation."

"I trust you."

In this, at any rate.

"Well, good. But another opinion might be needed for tax purposes since there is no track record from sales. If you have two or three independent appraisers giving you the same valuation, it will carry more weight with the IRS."

She held out her hand for the stack of notes on the clipboard.

"I can recommend some other appraisers if you like," she said.

Trace handed her the chipboard and moved to stand near the window, gazing out to the sea.

"This is the view he painted over and over, isn't it?"

"It seems to be," she said, stepping closer. "If you have any pull with your mother, I suggest you get her to view the paintings before the exhibit. I think she's going to be disappointed in what she sees and I hate for that discovery to be in a public venue."

"I have very little influence with my parents. But I'll tell her."

"Fine, then, I'm off."

He turned and looked at her. For a second Callie thought he was going to say something. Ask her to stay maybe?

"Thank you for the speedy work. Send me the bill, the estate will pay for your services."

She inclined her head. She looked around. It was unlikely she'd ever return to the cottage.

She reached into her pocket. "I have this for you."

She held out the key to the cottage and the sparkling diamond ring Tommy had given her and refused to take back.

Callie looked at the ring, feeling the weight of disappointment and betrayal. When he'd first given her this ring she'd been so full of hope.

She'd never expected to have it all tarnished and ruined within weeks. She'd taken it off and held it out to Tommy that horrible afternoon. But he'd refused to take it. He'd wanted to talk to her, but Callie wouldn't listen—not with that woman around.

Only, he'd died before they ever talked.

Not that mere talking would have changed anything. She knew that.

Trace looked at her. "Tommy would want you to keep the ring," he said.

Callie knew Trace believed everything had been perfect with their relationship. Would he be shocked to learn she had tried to return it to Tommy that afternoon, hurt and angry? The blonde standing in the bedroom doorway with the sheet wrapped partway around her had watched. What had she felt like when Tommy closed Callie's fingers around it and told her to keep it until she calmed down and they could talk?

Callie shivered, almost feeling the other in the room. She didn't care what that other woman had thought. She only cared that her heart had been broken that day.

She shook her head. "No."

"Why not?" Trace asked, his instincts obviously on alert.

"We aren't getting married. Let his estate have it. I have to go."

She put the two items in his outstretched hand and turned quickly. It would be a long time before she'd trust another man again after the way her supposedly devoted fiancé had cheated on her.

Trace held the ring in his hand, gazing at the sparkling diamond. The ring suited Callie, a simple solitaire. Why was she giving it back? He'd have thought a woman would keep the ring as a sentimental keepsake. He closed his fist around it.

He'd never found a woman to love. If he thought about it, one day he wanted a family. The kind where everyone loved each other and there were no favorites played. With the right woman, anything would be possible. It was finding her that might prove impossible.

Monday was the day the gallery was closed. Many other businesses in town were closed, as well. The weekenders had left and the locals knew better than to plan on shopping.

Callie liked working at the gallery those days because it was quiet. It gave her a chance to catch up on paperwork or give every painting and art piece a good dusting.

This Monday she'd partitioned off the alcove with screens and was trying to decide how best to display Tommy's work. Callie tried one layout and then another. She had to decide on the final arrangement of the paintings to get the lighting in place for best viewing advantage.

She had one wall done to her satisfaction when there was a knock on the front door. Couldn't the person see the Closed sign?

Callie peeked around the screen shocked when she saw the woman standing on the sidewalk, knocking again. She had wavy blond hair, makeup that looked overdone in the casual setting of Rocky Point. She wore very abbreviated shorts even for summer and a loose-fitting top, sliding off one shoulder. The last time Callie had seen her, she'd been wearing Tommy's sheet.

The woman cupped her hands against the glass and peered in. She saw Callie and motioned to the door.

Callie couldn't believe she was there, much less demanding to come in. Whatever in the world was the woman doing trying to enter the shop?

"I'm closed," she mouthed, pointing to the sign.

The woman rattled against the door, knocking again.

Sighing, Callie went to open. She didn't need this, but better to talk to her in private than have her shout something from the sidewalk. Just because shops were closed today, didn't mean people weren't out and about.

She unlocked the door. Standing so it couldn't be opened very wide, she said, "I'm closed today. Can you come another day?"

"I don't want to buy anything, I want to talk to you. And I'm only here today. Tomorrow I'm back at work."

She pushed against the door and Callie stepped to one side to allow her entry.

"Come with me," Callie said after she relocked the door. She led the way to her office, crossed to her desk and sat down. What in the world was this woman doing here?

"I'm Teresa Barrows," the woman said, looking around and sitting on one of the guest chairs. "You didn't know my name, I think. But you knew Tommy and I had something going on. I heard there's going to be a showing of Tommy's paintings."

She looked straight at Callie for confirmation.

"That's right. Friday is the opening and it'll be for five days."

"Are they worth a lot of money?"

Teresa was tall and slender. Her long legs were tanned and shown to advantage in the shorts. Her hair was long, wavy and swirling artfully around her face. She'd definitely appeal to men.

Callie was curious why she'd shown up at the gallery. To find out about the paintings? The advance publicity had listed times and dates in the newspaper.

"Art is valued on what people will pay. Nothing of Tommy's has ever sold, so I can only give an estimated value. My professional opinion has been given to the executor of his estate."

It really wasn't any of Teresa's business.

Plus Callie wouldn't divulge confidential information.

"I don't care about appraisals, what will they sell for?" the woman asked impatiently.

"The paintings aren't for sale," Callie said.

Why was the woman approaching her? Did she expect

something if the paintings sold? What claim would she have?

Callie was surprised to discover she felt very little either way about this person. She would have thought she'd be furious to meet her. But it was Tommy who earned her anger.

"If someone offers enough, everything's for sale," Teresa said, jumping up to pace the small space. "I need to know if they'll bring in some money. I went to Jocelyn Warren, but she wouldn't give me the time of day. You're my next hope."

Callie was shocked to hear she'd visited Jocelyn. What had she told the woman?

"What does it matter to you how much they are worth?" she asked, stalling. What was going on.

"Don't you recognize me?"

"You were with Tommy the day I found you both at the cottage."

Callie was proud of how calm her voice sounded. She could still picture Teresa standing in the doorway wrapped in the sheet. After she'd discovered them beneath those sheets together. Tommy had been contrite, apologetic. But no explanation he could have given would have changed the facts.

"No wonder he wanted me, you sound so cold and unconcerned. I miss him!"

"You of all people know our relationship changed dramatically that afternoon."

Callie felt inadequate. Teresa had tons more sex appeal

going for her. The contrast was dramatic. No wonder Tommy wanted her on the side. Would he have ever been satisfied in their marriage?

Now, for some reason Tommy's lover had sought her out. Curiosity demanded to know why.

"So again, I ask, why is any of this important?"

"I'm pregnant with his kid. And I want my share of his estate for the baby. I don't make enough to support a child. The Warrens are loaded. My baby deserves some of that money."

Callie stared at her. Teresa was carrying Tommy's baby? Good heavens. She was stunned with the news.

"Does Jocelyn know?" she asked.

"She thinks I'm trying some scam. I went there first. Sheesh, she's gonna be the baby's grandma. You'd have thought she'd be thrilled. Instead she accused me of lying. Get real, with the ease of DNA testing these days, who'd ever try to scam anyone? I hear Tommy's brother's in town. Twins have identical DNA so matching would be a snap. Maybe you should talk to her. She almost went bonkers when I did," Teresa said.

"She must have been surprised to learn what you had to say," Callie said slowly.

She couldn't imagine Jocelyn's reaction. The woman had no idea Tommy had been seeing Teresa. So much for keeping the secret so Jocelyn wouldn't be hurt.

"Duh! She went ballistic. I'm just asking for what's due Tommy's baby. How much is his stuff worth? His estate can give some to his child," Teresa said, glowering at Callie.

"Then you need to talk with Trace Warren. He's the executor of the estate."

Callie wondered if he had any inkling what was about to hit.

"He's staying at Tommy's cottage."

Teresa paced the small office. "Are you going to challenge it?"

"I have nothing to do with Tommy's estate, you know that. You were there when I ended the engagement," Callie said calmly.

For the first time she began to see things in a different light. Maybe God's hand had been in everything after all. She was thankful she'd found out when she did. What if she'd married him and Teresa showed up with a baby? She shivered at the thought.

"Yeah, well, don't think he was heartbroken. He was going to end it once you gave him a show. It was all for that. Anything to get his show. He'd have moved onto the big time and taken me with him once he sold his paintings," Teresa said with bravado.

"As I said, Trace is staying at the cottage. You should talk with him," Callie said. Had Tommy's interest in her been purely mercinary?

She refused to get into a discussion with Teresa.

Teresa stopped pacing and considered it.

"Not if he's going to give me the runaround like his mother did. You come with me."

"What? I'm not going with you."

"I need you as a witness. You can tell him Tommy and I

were an item. At least he'll have to pay attention. If he wants tests, I don't mind. But they have to pay for them. I'm not flush with cash like the Warrens are. I just want what's right for my baby."

Callie shook her head.

"I'll call Trace for you. Tell him you're coming," she offered.

It was more than she needed to do for Teresa. She couldn't believe the nerve of the woman, showing up here. Yet, if she'd been the one pregnant, wouldn't she do everything she could for her baby?

"I'm not going there alone. Who knows what a strange man would do? Especially if he reacts like his mom did," Teresa said petulantly.

"For heaven's sake, it's Tommy's brother. He isn't going to do anything but listen to you. Whether he does anything beyond that is up to him."

"Maybe the entire town needs to know that Tommy was cheating on you. How would you like that? " Teresa asked, glaring at Callie.

"I wouldn't like it at all. But it'd hurt his family more. The family that's also related to your baby," she said.

Had she kept quiet these weeks because of a desire to shield Jocelyn and Montgomery or to keep from becoming gossip herself?

For the first time, Callie wasn't sure some of her keeping quiet didn't stem from wanting to protect herself.

She had no idea what Teresa would do next. The best way to avoid rampant rumors all over town, was to get her taken care of. Callie didn't want the gossip and she was sure Jocelyn and Montgomery wouldn't, either.

"I said I could call."

"I want you there," Teresa said stubbornly. "I know you hate me, but if you ever cared for Tommy, you wouldn't want to hate his child."

"Not a very good argument. I don't hate you much less your child."

Callie shook her head. "Very well, I'll go to the cottage and talk to Trace. Do you have a car?" Callie asked, rising. Best to get it over with.

"Sure. I'll drive."

"I was thinking you could follow me over. That way you wouldn't have to bring me back here when we're finished," Callie said. The less time spent with Teresa the better.

"I guess that'd be all right," Teresa said.

In less than ten minutes Callie pulled into the driveway of the cottage. Only a couple of days ago she'd mentally said goodbye to all memories, good and bad. Never expecting to return, she certainly hadn't thought she'd be coming back with Tommy's pregnant lover.

"When's the baby due?" Callie asked after knocking on the door.

"Five months."

"So Tommy never knew," she said softly.

"Naw. And let me tell you it was a shock to me. At least it'll arrive in the fall. Tips aren't so great then 'cause the summer crowds are gone. Can you imagine me big as a house and trying to hustle tips?" Teresa said.

"Are you a waitress?"

"Cocktail waitress at the Blue Diamond Resort," she said, naming one of the larger ones in a nearby town.

Trace opened the door. For a moment he looked at Callie, then at Teresa.

"Something tells me I'm going to regret this, but won't you ladies come in?" he invited.

Chapter Twelve

Callie walked past him holding her head high, wishing she could say something to make it easier.

Teresa looked at Trace with speculation, the smile wide on her face.

"Well, don't you look just like Tommy. I mean, I knew you were twins, but seeing you in the flesh is quite the thing. It's like Tommy's still here."

She brushed against him as she entered, tilting her head almost flirtatiously. "I'm Teresa."

"A friend of Tommy's undoubtedly," Trace said, closing the door and regarding Teresa.

"A very close friend," she said with a wide smile.

He looked at Callie. "How do you know Teresa?"

"We never actually met formally before today. She came to the gallery to see me. I think you should listen to what she has to say."

"I'm pregnant with Tommy's baby," Teresa said bluntly.

Trace raised an eyebrow and studied her for another moment. "I probably should be shocked, but I'm only mildly surprised."

He looked at Callie again. "Did you know?"

She shook her head. "Teresa came to me because your mother didn't exactly embrace her with welcoming arms when she told her the news a little while ago."

"Knowing my mother, she undoubtedly called you a liar and told you never to try to besmirch the good name of her son," Trace said to Teresa.

"How did you know?" Teresa asked.

"It's happened before."

"It has?" Callie was startled.

"Old history. So what is it you want?" Trace asked.

"Some money to help raise this baby."

"As far as I know, Tommy didn't have any money," Trace said.

Teresa waved her hand around in an arc. "He had this place, that fancy car. He was an artist. His paintings must be worth something. He always said they were."

"This place is leased by my mother. The car was totaled, and my father held the insurance on it. And thus far the total appraisal of the paintings comes to very little. Of course, I would see that Tommy's child got a portion of his estate. But if you're looking for lots of cash, there isn't any."

"Don't give me that! He threw money around like it was water," Teresa protested. "What am I going to do if I can't get money? I don't make enough to raise a baby."

"He was a lavish spender," Callie added quietly.

"Then I don't know where he got the money. I've reviewed his tax records for the last few years, he didn't make enough to spend lavishly. Unless he was subsidized."

"What does that mean?" Teresa asked.

Her flirtatious attitude had faded. Now she became concerned, worried.

Callie almost felt sorry for her. Obviously she'd thought Tommy rich as could be and wanted a portion of the wealth for her baby.

"My mother probably gave him money to spend. Maybe she'll do the same for your baby."

"Not likely." Teresa looked at Trace and then at Callie. "She's already told me she thinks I'm a liar. If I have to, I'll get a lawyer and have him get me a share."

"I'd be happy to give you the name of Tommy's attorney. Yours could call him and they could hash it out," Trace said.

"You bet they can. A baby should get some of his father's estate."

Trace crossed to the dining room and grabbed a pad off the table. Jotting down the name and phone number, he handed the sheet to Teresa.

"Have your lawyer call Ben. He'll give him the facts. The estate hasn't been probated yet. We're still appraising the paintings. But they aren't going to bring in a lot of money."

"You're trying to make me believe that, but it won't work. After they go on sale at her gallery, they'll skyrocket in price. And that's when to sell. I'll be there to make sure I get my baby's share!"

She folded the paper and put it in her slim purse and flounced out the front door.

Callie looked after her wondering what was going to happen next.

"That was—enlightening," Trace said. "Did you know about her?"

"She's the one who left her clothes here I think," Callie said slowly. "I only found out about her a couple of days before Tommy died."

"How?"

She took a breath. "I came by and they were in bed together."

He swore. "You weren't expected, I take it."

"No. Tommy said it didn't mean anything. He wanted me to discuss the matter with him, but I said no."

"I see now why you don't want the engagement ring."

"It'd mean nothing. Just like it did when he gave it to me. She's four months pregnant, which means they were seeing each other at least a month or longer before he died. She said he only wanted me to get a showing at the gallery."

She tried to ignore what that did to her. Had Tommy had any regard for her at all? Was his attention all a ploy to get her to show his work in her gallery like Teresa said. With the backing of a prestige gallery behind him, had he hoped his paintings would become more valuable?

"I'm sorry," Trace said.

"Yeah, me, too."

"My mother didn't know?"

"I didn't tell anyone except Margo. He died so soon after I found out. There wasn't any reason to hurt your parents." Callie bit her lip. "I've been afraid I was the reason he crashed."

"If I remember the report correctly, he was loaded to the

gills with liquor, that was the reason he crashed."

"Drinking because I broke it off was my fear."

"With Teresa warming his bed, I doubt it."

Callie nodded, feeling hurt Trace would so quickly dismiss her impact on Tommy's life. "There isn't much else to say after that."

Callie headed for the door.

"I have to get back to the gallery."

She almost asked what Trace planned to do about Teresa, but decided she really didn't want to know. Tommy had made his choice and she'd made hers. The sooner she moved on, the better.

"Callie?"

She stopped at the door and looked back.

"Tommy let the better woman get away," he said.

She knew he was trying to make her feel better. She nodded and walked out.

But she wished for a moment that Trace had said more. Asked her to stay a little longer.

Trace watched as Callie drove away, then closed the door. What a mess his brother had caused. Had he really asked Callie to marry him as an entry into the gallery? Surely he had to know she had too much integrity to try to foist his work on the public at anything above its real value. Anything else wouldn't do her reputation as an art dealer any good.

But to be seeing another woman while engaged was beyond the pale. How could he do that?

Trace knew how. Tommy had gone through life as if it owed him. Nothing stuck. Trace wondered if some of the fault could be directed toward him. Hadn't he been getting his brother out of scrapes since school days? He'd known Tommy was the fair-haired son. He'd done his best to keep Tommy out of trouble, so his parents would find him of some worth, as well.

In retrospect, he hadn't done either of them any favors.

His parents expected him to rescue Tommy whenever he needed it. And by doing so, he'd never let Tommy learn valuable lessons which would have gone a long way to develop a stronger character.

Maybe his morals would never have been strong, but he might have been more circumspect about the feelings of others.

It made Trace feel almost sick to imagine how Callie must have felt that day, walking in to discover what she did.

He wished he knew how to protect her, to keep her safe from any hurt.

She'd been carrying that knowledge for months. He'd only just learned about it. If Tommy was around, he'd punch him in the nose.

Suzanne was in the gallery when Callie returned.

"What are you doing here?" Callie asked, surprised to see her on her day off.

"I came by to help get the alcove ready, I know you planned to work on the layout today. And to check out a rumor. Was there really some woman here who claims to be carrying Tommy's baby?"

"Where did you hear that?"

"At the market. Alice Rose was telling anyone who

would listen. She'd gotten it from the guy at the gas station when the woman asked directions. Lots of blond hair and very pretty, according to Alice Rose."

"She's dealing with Trace. He's handling the estate."

"Wish he'd handle my estate," Suzanne said. "He's yummy."

"He looks like Tommy."

"Ah, but there's a difference. You know that. They may look alike, but Trace is a lot steadier. More of a man, if you know what I mean."

"Like?"

"He likes women, don't get me wrong, but he's not here to charm our pants off, which I always thought was Tommy's goal in life."

"That's how you see them?"

"Trace's a man confident in his own self-worth. Tommy was narcissistic. And he was always on, if you know what I mean," Suzanne said.

"I do."

At the time it had bothered Callie a bit. She'd been thrilled with his attention, but sometimes felt overwhelmed by him. In retrospect, would he have always needed more reassurance than she could have given? Or was she thinking crazy. If he only wanted a showing, he'd never have married her. There had never been a long term relationship to lose.

Again she gave a short prayer for being delivered from a man who was not right for her.

Her cell phone rang as Callie entered her office.

"Hello?" she answered, placing her purse in a desk

drawer.

"Callie, my dear. How are you?" It was Jocelyn Warren.

"I'm well, Jocelyn. How are you?"

"Coping. It's not easy, is it?"

"What can I do for you?" Callie wasn't going to get sucked into Jocelyn's lamenting today. She'd had enough drama.

"Montgomery suggested we have dinner together Thursday evening. It seems like ages since we all got together. And it will give us one last time together before the show."

"I don't know," Callie stalled. She didn't wish to see the Warrens anytime soon.

"I'll have Trace pick you up at seven. He's staying at Tommy's cottage, you know. So helpful to have him packing away Tommy's things. I simply couldn't bear it."

If Trace was going, it'd be easier to deal with the others.

"All right, Thursday at seven."

Was Jocelyn going to ignore Teresa? Callie didn't know how to bring it up without sounding like she was seeking gossip. After another minute of conversation, she hung up feeling sympathy for Jocelyn. It has to be so hard to lose a child, no matter what the age.

And to find him less than perfect would hurt even more.

Yet Jocelyn had another son. Maybe she should be a bit more grateful for that son.

Not that it was Callie's place to determine their family loyalties. Today had been too awkward. She couldn't wait to escape the cottage. Did he feel as disconcerted with Teresa's news? Or didn't men feel the same way?

When the cottage phone rang Trace answered it knowing it had to be his mother, no one else had a reason to call.

"I've invited Callie to dinner Thursday evening. Would you please pick her up at seven? We need to discuss the showing," his mother said without greeting. "I also want to make it clear to her that we still regard her as family. She almost married your brother, you know."

Trace knew full well that to his mother Callie represented part of the shrine to Tommy's memory. What did she think about Teresa?

He asked.

"Do not speak to me about that–that floozy. She's trying to cash in on Tommy's fame. I don't for a minute believe she's pregnant, much less with Tommy's child. She's too slim. If she thinks she can extort us into giving her money, she's in for a rude awakening."

"There are DNA tests that can prove or disprove without a doubt," he mentioned.

"Ha, let her try. We'll call her bluff. That is not the purpose of dinner. Please do not bring her name up when Callie is here. This is a family dinner. I want it to go smoothly."

Trace's instincts went on alert. "Family?"

"Your father, me and Tommy's brother with Tommy's fiancé."

So that was it. She was trying to force a role on him different from what she suspected. He could alleviate all her worries by telling her Callie only saw him as a stand-in for Tommy. It was not a role he'd take.

"I'll pick her up at seven," he said.

When he finished his conversation with his mother, he called the attorney to alert him to the new development. Trace laid out his terms—before any negotiations were started, he wanted DNA proof Teresa's baby was Tommy's.

Physicians might not take samples from in utero fetuses, so they may have to wait until after Teresa delivered. Trace planned to let the attorney deal with all that. He had enough on his plate.

He leaned back in the chair and looked around the room his brother had used as an office. He'd been going through all the papers here putting them in some sort of order, tossing what wasn't needed, organizing those that were. Paying any bills still outstanding. It was a thankless task, but one that needed doing.

He reached for a large wooden box near the desk, surprised to find it heavy. Opening it, Trace saw a stack of papers—all covered with black pen-and-ink drawings. He picked up several and looked at them.

The top three were of Teresa, in various stages of undress. One was of Callie looking pensive. A couple of portraits of people he didn't recognize. One of his father working on a marble sculpture.

These were excellent. Why had Tommy wasted time on mediocre oil paintings when he could capture nuances and emotions so well in this medium?

Trace began laying the papers out on the cluttered desk.

There was no one subject, like with his painting. These ranged from portraits, to evocative scenes from around Rocky Point, to drawings of old and gnarled hands, working on repairing a fishing net.

He dialed Callie's gallery. The phone rang and rang. Checking his watch, Trace noted it was after six. She was undoubtedly home. He started to call her cell.

Stopping, he decided he'd take the pictures to her. She could tell him more about them if she actually saw them rather than hear his description over the phone.

It was not an excuse to see her.

It sure felt like one.

He didn't care. He wanted to make sure she was doing all right after today's revelations. As Tommy's brother, didn't he have a family responsibility to watch out for her?

Carefully restacking the pictures, he placed them in the box and headed out. All but the ones of Teresa. He wasn't showing those to anyone.

Chapter Thirteen

Even as Trace knocked on the door to Callie's flat, he had second thoughts. He could have waited until morning and taken them into the gallery to ask for a formal appraisal.

Callie opened the door. She'd changed into shorts and a cropped top. Her hair was piled up on her head to bare her neck. Her feet were bare. For a moment Trace forgot why he'd come. She looked young and carefree and pretty. He had a hard time remembering she was off-limits.

"Hi, Trace, I didn't expect to see you again today," she said. "Is there a problem?"

"Not exactly. I wanted your opinion on something," he said, holding up the box. "I found these."

"Come in. What's in the box?"

He put the box on the dining table and removed the lid.

"Oh, my," she said, reaching for the top drawing.

A pensive pen-and-ink drawing of Callie gazing over the sea was on top. She studied it for a long moment. Then putting it down beside the box, she turned over the papers, one by one, laying them on top of the table as she withdrew them from the box.

"I never saw these," she murmured. "Oh, isn't this great of Peter." She indicated a fisherman at the dock. More and more sheets were picked up.

"These are amazing. I knew he did pen-and-ink sometimes. He always had a pad handy, said it kept him in the mood. But I only saw a couple before this. I have the one he gave me. I had no idea he had so many. These are wonderful."

She pulled out a chair and sat, forgetting Trace was even in the room as she happily took one sketch after another and held it up for perusal. Soon she began sorting them. He sat and watched her, fascinated by the intensity with which she studied each picture. She hadn't been anywhere near this excited about Tommy's paintings.

"They're good," he said when she reached the bottom of the box.

"Oh, Trace, they're wonderful. Look at the variety. He was especially good at portraitures. You don't know most of the people here, but I do and Tommy captured not only their likeness, but something of their personalities, as well. Why didn't he tell me he was doing these?"

"I have no idea. But there are well over a hundred in this box."

"Did you look for others?" she asked, looking up at him.

"No. Do you think there're more?"

"I don't know. I didn't know about these. But if so, we need to appraise them. These will sell well, I know it. They won't command as much as an oil painting by a proven artist, but they'll sell better than dockside paintings, which is what his oils would go for."

"I think I'll need to have them all sell. Things have changed as of today."

"You mean Teresa?"

"Who else?"

"Are you going to make sure the baby's Tommy's?" she asked.

"I've already talked to the attorney about it. But I don't have any doubts."

Callie looked at the stacks she'd made. "I don't, either. It's so sad. How could he have crashed his car if he was going to become a father?"

"He didn't know. You heard Teresa," Trace said. "Besides, I doubt if knowing would have changed anything."

"He might have done things differently. He could have married her," Callie said.

Trace shook his head. "I don't believe he would have married Teresa. Not once mother got a look at her."

"Your mother didn't run his life."

"To an extent she did–she provided the money. He wouldn't risk cutting that off."

"He could have gotten a job to support himself," she said with some asperity.

"If he wanted to do that, he'd have done so before now. Teresa was one of many beautiful blondes he liked to date."

"What happened other times?"

"Nothing important. I can't believe no matter what, our conversations always lead back to Tommy. I feel he's sitting right between us at every instant," Trace said in frustration.

"He's the reason we met," she said.

"For once I'd like to have a conversation without him. Just you and me."

"We have. Contrary to what you think, Tommy's not at the forefront of my mind. He hasn't been since I found him and Teresa. I didn't confuse you two the other night." There, she'd told him again. *Please, let him listen and hear, Lord.*

Trace didn't say anything for a moment, then he pointed to the drawings. "Good enough for the retrospective?"

"Absolutely! Good grief, I'm supposed to give the final okay for the brochure to the printer tomorrow. I need to select which of these I want to display and write a description and set a price. If you want pricing on all of the ones on display, I'll have to do that, as well. I hope I can get it done before he closes tomorrow. It's cutting it close, but I don't know how else to get it all in. These are too good to leave out. And if your decision to raise money holds, we need to assign a value on the other displayed pieces and see if they'll sell, too."

"Let me help."

She tilted her head slightly looking at him. She nodded.

"Okay. You don't know any of these people so you won't be influenced that way. Pick out the twelve ones you like best as if you are a potential customer. Ones that you'd buy."

"That's not very scientific."

"Actually it is. You know what you like. I'll check behind you to see if they really hold potential."

They worked together for more than an hour. It was

growing late when they stopped.

"I could do an entire exhibit on the pen-and-ink," she said, taking the dozen they'd selected to show. "Maybe later in the summer, if these sell well, I could do a special," she said. She had never done a pen and ink showing. Sometimes she had one or two mixed in with the paintings and sculptures on display. She'd be willing to try it for a week.

She carefully stacked the papers and put them back in the box.

"I can't appraise these right away," she said.

"No rush, as it turns out. I need to raise as much money from the estate as I can. Teresa's baby is my niece or nephew."

Callie smiled. "That's right, you'll be the baby's uncle. And your folks will be grandparents. Do you think they'll like that idea when they get used to it?"

"No."

She looked surprised.

Trace knew she'd be delighted at the thought of a new baby in the family. Why hadn't Tommy snapped her up when he had the chance?

"It'll be competition. One thing about my parents, they're very competitive for attention. You know that, you work with them."

"I see them in a different light as artists. I never thought about how your home life was."

"It was different from my friends, but it was the only family I knew. They aren't bad parents, just narrow in their focus," Trace said.

He'd accepted long ago that his parents were as they were. It saved a lot of tension in the long run. They'd never change. He no longer wanted them to.

He rose and pushed in his chair. "I'll leave the box with you. Let me know if you need help when appraising. I'm good at taking notes."

"You're good at a few other things, as well," she murmured, looking up at him.

He could see the interest in her eyes. For a moment he let himself remember how she'd felt in his arms, her mouth against his. How he wished he could sweep her away to learn every thing there was to know about her and count the world well lost.

However much he wanted that, it wasn't going to happen.

She still saw him as Tommy.

No matter what she said, she was disappointed in his brother, hurt in a deeply personal way by his betrayal. Yet despite it all, she'd called for Tommy.

The next morning Callie woke early. She'd had trouble sleeping through the night as she realized time was moving swiftly and Trace'd be leaving soon. Tossing and turning hadn't done anything but keep her awake. She didn't know anything she could do to change things.

Finally she prayed about the entire situation. Peace descended and she was able to sleep through the last couple of hours before time to wake up.

She dressed for the day, then fixed a light breakfast.

While eating, she began jotting down descriptions for the newly discovered drawings. She was more excited about these than all the other paintings she'd seen. She knew exactly which frames she'd use to highlight the stark black-and-white sketches.

Once satisfied, she headed for the gallery to type up the new descriptions on the computer to get them off to the printer's as soon as possible. Next she'd need to decide where she would place them on the walls. Maybe grouped together on the back wall of the alcove. Or would scattered through the collection be better?

By the time Suzanne arrived shortly before ten, Callie had the retrospective program ready to go except for pricing. She took the draft and walked into the alcove, looking at the pictures, assigning a value that would be used as a start for negotiations.

She'd let Trace know he'd likely need to be willing to come down at least ten percent. But hold firm beyond that. Many times patrons offered full price.

She finished assigning prices, labeled how she'd hang the pen-and-ink drawings and gave the entire draft to Suzanne to take to the printer's. She wanted to get started framing the new drawings as soon as Suzanne returned.

For the first time, she looked forward to the retrospective rather than dreading it.

Callie spent most of the day working on the framing, finishing around four. Satisfied, she hurried to the alcove to hang them. Rearranging the others took longer than she expected and it was closing time before she finished.

"Want me to wait until you're ready to leave?" Suzanne asked as she locked the main doors.

"No, run along. I won't be much longer," she said, hanging another picture in the exact spot that would highlight it the best.

It turned out to be later than she thought when she was finally satisfied. The printer promised to have the booklet back Friday morning. Now all that was needed was to confirm the refreshments by the caterer. She was using Marcie's again, and knew the hors d'oeuvres would taste delicious and be presented most elegantly.

Heading for home, she swung by the café for a quick meal. To her surprise Trace sat alone at one of the tables on the deck, his dinner half eaten. She went to join him.

"Mind if I sit here?" she asked.

He looked up and gestured to the empty chair. "Glad for the company."

The deck was half-full with families and couples. The setting sun provided a blaze of colored clouds against the darkening landscape.

"You're eating late," he said once she ordered.

"I just finished up the display for the show. The brochure information was delivered to the printer and now only the lighting remains."

"Need any help with that?"

"Thanks for the offer, but we can manage. I'm hoping everything's ready to go at the day before the opening. I hate being rushed. What did you do today?"

"I finished going through the office papers. Trashed a

lot. Organized the rest and turned them over to the attorney. Fortunately Tommy seemed to have kept up with his bills. Nothing was in arrears and there were no big surprises. I looked for another box of drawings, but didn't find one in the house, but there was one in the garage. I think they're older. Some of the pages are yellowed as if with age."

"Are they as good as the ones I saw?" she asked.

"I think so. If I'd known I was going to see you tonight, I'd have brought them with me. I can bring them by tomorrow if you like."

Callie nodded. "Or I can stop by and pick them up."

She didn't want to talk about Tommy. Could she change the subject? Here was a perfect chance to show Trace she was not confusing him with his brother. She liked talking with him. Liked him period!

"I'm leaving tomorrow for a couple of days in Boston," Trace said. "Checking in with the office and then visiting a couple of old friends. I'll be back Thursday afternoon. The infamous Warren family dinner, you know."

She nodded, feeling let down.

Her meal was served. For the next few minutes Callie was silent as she began her dinner. Trace had finished his. Would he stay until she was also finished?

Tommy's show began on Friday and would run for a week. She hoped Trace would stay the entire time. Maybe she could tell him he needed to be available to negotiate any sales.

"I'm glad you're staying longer than originally planned," she said. "I hear the weather is supposed to stay beautiful for another week."

Great, she was resorting to banalities.

"As long as it isn't a tropical downpour it's good in my book these days. We get daily showers in the Amazon Basin," he said.

They talked a little longer about the vagaries of the weather. Trace stayed to keep her company. She hoped for an invitation to go for a walk or something, but as soon as she finished, he made preparations to leave.

"If you're leaving in the morning, maybe I should run by tonight and get that other box. Save you time tomorrow," she said.

It was still light out, early enough to stop by without making it seem like a big deal.

"Fine. I'll follow you there," he said.

Callie took a second once in her car to run a brush through her hair and recolor her lips. She looked a little tired from lack of sleep, not that Trace noticed.

"Come in, it won't take me a second to get the box," Trace said, throwing open the front door when they reached the cottage.

"I'm in no hurry," Callie said, walking into the living room.

It no longer looked like the same place she'd visited during her engagement. The curtains were wide-open, as were the windows. The evening breeze swept through, giving a crisp freshness to the room. A briefcase lay opened on the coffee table, stacks of reports, photographs and even a small rolled cylinder of paper rested beside several pens and pencils, makeshift paperweights holding them on the table.

She walked over while Trace went to the back of the cottage. One stack of papers looked to be spreadsheets with columns of numbers. Another stack was of photographs. What caught her attention was the top one. It was of a bridge—or a portion of one.

She sat on the sofa and picked up the stack. Shuffling through them, she could see each stage captured as building progressed—clearing the banks on either side of the river; the pouring of foundations; the initial steel beams jutting from the shore. As she moved through them, she didn't need the dates at the corner of each one to see the progression.

Soaring against the deep blue sky, with thick green foliage surrounding the site, the structure was a study in contrasts. The bridge looked mammoth from snapshots taken close up. But from the distance on the river it looked almost lacy—and beautiful.

"Here's the other box," Trace said, coming back into the living room.

"These are amazing," she said, holding up the photographs. "I kept them in order. These are of the bridge you're building, aren't they?"

"Yes. I usually take pictures as we go. A chronology of events, so to speak."

"It's a lovely structure. This one must have been taken just before you left," she said, holding out one showing half the span. The date was four days before she'd first met him.

Trace put down the box and sat next to her. "It was. I brought it home in case my folks wanted to see it."

Callie would bet the gallery they hadn't even asked.

"Tell me about each one," she said, holding out the photographs and leaning back.

Trace took them and began a brief description of the different stages they'd already completed. He made the site come alive and she soon had a better appreciation of how dangerous the work was, how frustrating dealing with red tape and bureaucratic delays. She gained a new appreciation for the man who patiently fought through all the snafus to get the bridge built. When he unrolled some of the plans she could see how the finished bridge would look.

"Take a picture with the sun glinting on it and the sky so blue. It'd make a terrific study. I could sell it," she said, already envisioning the finished photograph, matted with a silver frame.

She didn't carry photographs in her gallery, but had several friends who did. She already had a buyer for Trace's picture of the finished bridge–herself. Besides the beauty it represented, it'd be a tie to a man she was finding more and more fascinating.

When he wound down, he glanced out the window, surprised to see the darkness. Checking his watch, he shook his head.

"I talked your ear off. It's after ten."

"The time flew by. I can't believe how dangerously you live. Beyond the basics of falling off the structure, or getting hit in the head by a swinging steel girder, there's disease, lack of hygiene and nutritious foods, insects, snakes." Callie shivered thinking about how many ways Trace could be injured or become ill.

"You make it sound worse than it is. I'm healthy and careful. We all are on the site. There were fewer than twenty injuries last year. Since we have so many unskilled laborers working for us, and a language barrier, that's pretty remarkable."

Callie thought Trace was pretty remarkable, but knew he didn't want to hear that.

She rose and picked up the box of Tommy's sketches, hugging them to her.

"Thanks for taking the time to explain so much. I really enjoyed hearing about the bridge. Does it have a name?"

"Not so far. We call it project J-173." He rose and stood near her.

Callie felt her senses go on alert. They were so close.

"I'll walk you out to your car," he said.

The night was black, few lights around. The cottages farther along the road were dark. The air was still warm, though the breeze cooled it down from the heat of the day.

He stopped by the car and Callie turned, leaning against the car for a moment, the box still in her arms.

"I enjoyed tonight, Trace," she said.

"I did, too. It's not often I get to discuss my work."

"Too bad, you'd make a great lecturer. Maybe you should give travelogue talks between jobs, showing pictures of the work, and some of the local settings."

He half laughed. "I'm not that interesting, merely an engineer who loves his work."

"And takes justifiable pride in it."

He didn't respond right away. The silence grew.

"Callie," he said softly.

She held her breath until he leaned over to kiss her.

Chapter Fourteen

Callie felt the magic of his touch. She wished she could drop the box of sketches and throw her arms around him. But she dared not do that.

Trace threaded his fingers through her hair, his palms cradling her cheeks. He took his time kissing her. Callie felt she was floating. Blood pounded in her veins, her skin felt too tight. She wanted more, to feel his body against hers. To explore, touch, learn.

After endless moments of sheer delight, he pulled back giving light kisses along her jaw, across her cheeks.

"You are so sweet," he said softly.

Finally he stood, releasing her and reaching to open the car door.

"Drive safely home," he said.

She couldn't speak, only nod. Tossing the box onto the seat, she almost reached out for another kiss, but thought better of it. She didn't want anything to mar this special moment and she was afraid if she pushed for more, he'd back off.

As he watched her drive away, Trace called himself every kind of fool there was. He'd been tempted beyond his ability to resist kissing her. He was lucky to hold on to the belief she liked kissing him. At least this time she hadn't called him by his brother's name.

There was no future here. He had a bridge site to return to and another one on the horizon when this one was completed. His mother believed his interest in Callie was a carryover from the rivalry of their younger days. Who knew what Callie believed? He was not about to ask her.

Turning back to the cottage, Trace was glad he was leaving tomorrow. Being in Boston would give him some distance to gain perspective. When he returned and went to the family dinner, he'd be able to play the part of Tommy's brother. And keep any interest in Callie a secret.

He entered and saw the photographs and construction drawings spread across the table. She'd been fascinated, he'd recognized that. A novelty after so many artistic types, he bet.

Slowly he gathered everything up and replaced them in his briefcase. Maybe he'd look up an old girlfriend in Boston and take her out to dinner.

Anything to get beyond the idea of becoming involved with Callie Miller.

At six fifty-five on Thursday, Callie was pacing her flat. Trace was supposed to pick her up any minute. She hadn't spoken with him since leaving his cottage the other evening. She was surprised how eager she was to see him again. She'd done nothing but think about that kiss in the days since. Every time he touched her, she felt a tingle of electricity.

More and more she daydreamed about the two of them

becoming a couple. If only the specter of Tommy didn't ruin every idea she had. Still the fantasy had kept her awake long into the nights.

Would he ever forgive her faux pas of calling him his brother's name?

More and more Callie was having trouble remembering Tommy. He seemed like a person she'd known long ago. And not very well as it turned out.

Trace filled her thoughts these days.

The knock on the door came right at seven.

Another thing she liked about the man. He was punctual. As a businessperson, she appreciated that.

"Hello," she said, her heart fluttering when she saw him.

He looked terrific in the casual shirt and neatly pressed khakis.

"Ready?" His eyes lit in appreciation, but he said nothing.

Disappointed, she nodded, picking up the plate of cookies she'd prepared for the Warrens.

"I made some snicker doodles. I hope your parents will like them."

"If they don't I sure do. Maybe I should hope they don't. You'd then have to give them to me," he teased lightly as they walked to his rental car.

"I'm happy to make you a batch all for yourself," she responded. "How was Boston?"

"Great as always. I saw some old friends. Did some work at the office there. Our headquarters are in New York, but we have offices in several major cities. Is everything set for the opening of the show tomorrow?"

"Yes. The booklets arrived this morning, a day early. They came out perfect. I hope you and your parents will be pleased."

She'd been startled when she'd received the finished version and looked at the picture she'd chosen of Tommy to grace the front. It looked so much like Trace, she felt confused. The same smile, same twinkle in his eyes when amused.

But she could see the differences, as well. Tommy's jaw was not as strong as Trace's. His face still looked boyish while Trace's was definitely all man. He'd matured, Tommy was forever young.

Callie had been to the Warren's home several times, first as a representative of the gallery and then as Tommy's fiancé. The last time had been shortly after the funeral when she and Jocelyn planned the retrospective.

The house looked much the same, except the yard and garden seemed neglected. Of course it was high summer, everything looked a tad wilted with the heat. Still, Callie was surprised to see it less than pristine.

Jocelyn threw wide the door when they walked up the path.

"Oh, Callie, it's been too long. You know you're to treat this as your home," she said, gathering her in a warm embrace. "Come in. Trace, thanks for picking her up."

"Some cookies," Callie said, handing Jocelyn the platter.

"Aren't you sweet! You know how much Montgomery and I love cookies."

Jocelyn took the platter and escorted them inside the house.

Callie noticed Jocelyn didn't extend the same kind of welcoming hug to Trace. Why not? she wondered.

Montgomery was in the living room. He rose when they entered.

"Good to see you again, Callie. Trace. How was Boston?"

"What would everyone like to drink?" Jocelyn asked. "Trace, how long were you in Boston? Did you date any pretty girls while you were there? You need to date when you can. Being in the wilds of Brazil certainly gives you no chance to see women."

Callie looked at Jocelyn, then at Trace. She noticed the slight tightening of his jaw at his mother's comment.

"As a matter of fact, I took Susan Waters out for dinner last night. Remember her from our college days?" he asked, avoiding Callie's gaze.

She looked away quickly.

He'd taken someone else out for dinner.

Fine. There was no understanding between them.

But the dart of jealousy surprised her. She was not getting interested that way in Tommy's brother! She was not!

Except that extraordinary kiss she couldn't forget. Had he kissed Susan Waters like that?

Callie frowned, not wanting to picture that scenario. She felt suddenly awkward–like an unwanted fifth wheel.

"How nice. You should invite her for a visit. Now, while Montgomery gets the drinks, you come with me, Callie. I've finished my tribute to Tommy and want you to see it. If you like it, I want you to show it at the gallery," Jocelyn said, taking Callie's arm gently and leading her toward the studio.

Callie followed Jocelyn from the house to one of two studios that had been built in the backyard. Montgomery's was larger, with a roll-up door that enabled large slabs of stone to be brought in for his sculpting. Jocelyn's studio was comprised of mostly windows, with an expanse on the north wall that was all double-pane glass.

Trace went with them, though Callie thought he'd stay to talk with his father.

Jocelyn dramatically threw open the door and gestured to the large canvas on an easel that faced them.

Callie stepped inside and slowly crossed the room to study the painting.

It was beautiful, haunting and sad.

Jocelyn had captured a garden with weeping flowers, a weeping willow tree to the left. In the right lower corner a figure with white hair, bent over as if in inconsolable grief. A discarded teddy bear lay on the grass at her feet. The colors were vibrant and compelling.

At first glance it was a beautiful garden in full blossoms and colors. Closer inspection showed all the flowers drooping slightly, as if in sadness. Everything was slightly blurred, as if seen through tears.

The overall feeling was one of utter grief and despair. Yet the colors were vibrant, the entire scene reminiscent of the impressionists.

How had she managed that? It was what made her one

of America's leading painters. Collectors would be thrilled with this latest work.

"It's beautiful. Maybe one of your very best," she said, feasting on the nuances she picked up the longer she studied it.

"It was cathartic. I needed to expunge my deepest grief. But I don't want to see it again. It was enough to do," Jocelyn said, looking out the window.

Callie knew it would bring top dollar, but she herself wouldn't want such a sad painting in her home. Maybe because she knew exactly what caused the painting.

"It's beautiful, Mother," Trace said. "Tommy would've loved it."

"I hope so," she said sadly. "It's my tribute to my precious son."

Dinner was served on the patio, sheltered from the evening breeze. Jocelyn had prepared a ham and potatoes and cabbage meal, served with both red wine and iced tea.

"It was Tommy's favorite," Jocelyn said as she served Callie's plate.

Callie remembered. Every time she'd eaten at the Warrens with Tommy, Jocelyn had served the same meal.

She glanced at Trace suspecting this was not his favorite meal. Had his parents served his favorite his first night home?

"What's your favorite?" she asked him.

"New England clam chowder, lobster and crusty bread," Montgomery said unexpectedly.

Trace looked at his father in surprise. "I didn't know

you'd remember."

Montgomery returned his son's look and nodded. Glancing at Jocelyn, he commented, "We will have that one night before you leave."

"Chowder's so hard to prepare," Jocelyn said as she began to eat. "It's difficult to keep the milk from curdling."

"No more difficult than any other meal you prepare, my dear," Montgomery said. "I wouldn't mind some fresh lobster myself. It's been a long time since we've had any. Why live here if we don't take advantage?"

"We live here for more than food," Jocelyn said with some asperity. "I'm sure Trace is glad for any home-cooked meal, working in such outlandish places as he does."

"Speaking of that," Callie said. "Have you seen the pictures he brought home of the bridge they're building? It's really amazing."

Jocelyn and Montgomery looked at her with puzzlement.

"What pictures?" Montgomery asked.

"The ones he takes of the construction, at each stage. Trace's done that for each job he's worked on," Callie said, looking at him for confirmation.

He nodded, glancing at his parents.

"Why?" Jocelyn asked looking confused.

"To document the different processes and steps in the building. And to capture the feeling of the place where they're being built. The photographs I saw the other evening really gave me a feeling for the challenge of the job. It's not as if they're in downtown Boston with everything close at hand. They're hundreds of miles up the Amazon River with each item, tool, food, everything having to be brought up on barge or boat. Or along the dirt road that the bridge will connect."

Montgomery smiled slightly as he listened to Callie. "Indeed?"

"Many of the men working there are thousands of miles from home. The only communications they have is via computer—when the generators are running to provide electricity, and if the wireless feature's working. They're gone for months at a time. In dangerous circumstances, hot weather, no amenities that we take for granted." Callie wanted his parents to understand. How could they not be interested in their other son?

Jocelyn looked perplexed. "Is that true, Trace?"

"Pretty much," he said.

"I had no idea." She looked at her son as if he were an alien species.

"You would if you asked him about his job," Callie said with annoyance. These people had a wonderful man for a son and seemed to completely ignore him.

"I've never quite understood why anyone would do such a thing," Jocelyn said.

"I enjoy building," Trace said. He looked amused when he met Callie's gaze. "And I've never had such an ardent advocate before."

"You've accomplished a lot. And the things you've built will last long after you're gone," she said. "Think how much you are helping people you'll never meet. Monuments of steel."

"Like a sculpture?" Montgomery asked.

"You could say Trace sculpts with steel," Callie murmured.

"You make it sound artistic. It's just a bridge," Jocelyn said.

"No, it's not just a bridge. You should see it, it's beautiful, or will be when finished. I've asked for photographs."

"Whatever for?" the older woman asked.

"To sell, of course. I don't normally sell photographs, but in this case will make an exception."

She had not known she was going to say that. From the startled look on all three faces, no one else had expected that, either.

But, darn it, she wanted Trace to get some interest or respect or something from his family. Didn't they realize what a special man he was? That what he was doing was important!

"I can't believe I'm hearing you say that, Callie," Jocelyn said. "After all the times Tommy tried to get you to exhibit his work and you refused. Now you're talking about showing a bunch of pictures? Of a construction site?"

Callie fell silent. She couldn't argue that point. More than once in public Tommy had tried to cajole her into giving him the showing he wanted. They had fought over that issue several times.

At the time, she'd pleaded with him to stop asking, but he seemed to think causing a confrontation in public would have her give in more easily. He'd learned that didn't work.

Would he have ever given up and ended their engagement?

"There's a difference," she said at last.

"And that being?" Jocelyn was not willing to give her the benefit of the doubt, Callie knew that.

"Photographs would be quite different," Trace said, breaking into the tension. "Tommy would have needed to compete with artists of your caliber for a showing at her gallery. Any pictures she chose to show would have little or no competition, and would be solely for the novelty aspect."

"It's not art," Jocelyn said.

"I think there would be a market for it," Callie said. "Not the same collectors who buy your paintings, but there are lots of people who prefer photographs to paintings. It's not a market I've branched into, but I might. If Trace delivers the pictures."

"Trace is not an artist. Not like Tommy was."

"Jocelyn," Callie said gently. "You need to come see the paintings before the opening tomorrow night."

"It's going to be hard enough to be there at all. I need the fortification of friends and neighbors."

"Is there a problem?" Montgomery asked. "This is not the first time you've tried to get us to see the paintings."

"I think you'll both be disappointed. Tommy wasn't up to Jocelyn's caliber," she said diplomatically.

"He had talent. Once the retrospective has been reviewed, appreciation for his work will grow. He had such potential. I can't bear to think it's gone forever."

"He didn't live up to what promise he showed as a kid, Mom," Trace said gently.

"How dare you denigrate your brother's work! You're nothing but an engineer, what do you know about art? You were jealous of Tommy as children, as teenagers and still are, as far as I can tell. Are you making cozy with Callie trying to win her over–take her away from your brother? It won't work, she'll see through you in an instant! She loved Tommy. He was an artist. She runs an art gallery. It was a perfect match."

"Tommy's dead. Even if I wanted to take anything of his, what would it matter? He'd never know," Trace said reasonably.

"But you'd believe you finally beat him. Would that make you feel like the better man?" Jocelyn was getting carried away.

Callie wanted to say Trace didn't need to do anything to be the better man, but wisely kept quiet. The evening was fast getting out of hand and she didn't want to do anything to make it worse.

"Be warned, Callie, Trace and Tommy had a fierce rivalry all their lives. He may seem interested in you now, but it's only because Tommy was," Jocelyn said spitefully.

"As children maybe they were competitive, but I hardly think they'd be so now. As far as I can tell, Trace hasn't been around for the last decade. Hardly conducive to continued rivalry," Callie said, trying to interject some calmness into the conversation.

"He was always jealous of his brother," Jocelyn said.

"Hardly fair, Jocelyn," Montgomery said. "As children they were in and out of scrapes, but Trace hasn't competed with his brother in any way over the last decade. They couldn't be more dissimilar despite being twins. And from where I'm sitting, Trace has far more to be jealous of than Tommy did. He's become a success in a very competitive field. Remarkable in and of itself, but he did without any help from us. He hasn't asked us for a dime since he began his junior year in college."

The statement needed no further explanation. Tommy had been subsidized all along by his mother and everyone there knew it.

Chapter Fifteen

Callie began to count the seconds until she could escape. She marveled that Trace could keep his calm and talk easily with his father after his mother's scathing comments. If she ever had children, Callie vowed, she'd never play favorites.

At last the lengthy meal ended.

"I have to get home. I need to be up early tomorrow to put the finishing touches on the exhibit. We close at six as normal and then we reopen at seven o'clock for the reception. I'd love you to see the paintings before the general public, Jocelyn." Callie had to try once more. "If only to see if I've priced them competitively."

Jocelyn raised an eyebrow. "Priced them. I said they weren't for sale."

Callie took a deep breath and looked at Trace for guidance. He came to her rescue.

"I told her to price them and sell them if she can. Circumstances have changed in the last few days. The estate may need as much money as it can bring in."

"I said they weren't for sale." Jocelyn would brook no interference with her decree.

"You can buy them if you want to keep them, Mom. It's not as if some of the money wouldn't be distributed back to you," Trace said.

"It's the principle of the thing," she said. "He was my son. His work should stay in the family."

"He was our son and you've often said he needed to get his work out into the world so people would appreciate his talent," Montgomery said. "Let's see what happens."

Callie met Trace's gaze. They knew the world would never appreciate the work as Jocelyn imagined.

"Thank you for dinner, Mom. Dad, it was good to talk with you," Trace said, rising. He wasn't one to mess around. It was past time to leave.

Callie added her thanks and quickly got up to follow him.

Once in the car, backing from the driveway, Callie turned to him.

"Are your family dinners always this exciting?"

"This was mellow. My mother hasn't quite grasped the meaning of tact."

Callie felt suddenly grateful for the love in her own family. Her parents didn't understand her desire to live by the sea, but they supported her in every way they could. She always knew she was loved for being herself.

"Thanks for coming to bat for me," Trace said. "Novel experience. I can't remember when someone stood up for me before. Except once in college."

"What happened then?"

"Not much, a case of mistaken identity. A friend

vouched for me and the matter was closed."

She knew there was more to the story, but if he didn't want to share it with her, she wouldn't push. Their relationship was too fragile to stand up to any demands. If they had a relationship.

Jocelyn certainly had done her best to nip any inclinations that way in the bud.

And what about that woman he'd seen in Boston?

Her optimism dimmed. Trace had never given her any hint of a future. He'd said how much he loved his job. And she didn't have the kind of career that would allow her to pack up to follow him to the remote outreaches of the world.

"Anything I can do to help with the exhibit tomorrow?" Trace asked.

"Just lend moral support when I open the doors at seven," she said.

She was growing more and more nervous as the time approached. She wanted the showing to go well, but knew she couldn't count on anything. Patrons of the arts were sometimes fickle. They could make or break an exhibit with the most off the wall reasons.

"I'll be leaving the end of next week. By then we'll have an idea of how the sales go. Once you give me the pen-and-ink drawing appraisals for tax purposes, we can begin winding up the financial part of the estate. Any paintings that sell for more, I'll just pay the extra tax. Would you take me sailing once more before I leave?"

Callie looked at him in surprise. She smiled. She'd love

to!

"How about Monday? It's a free day for me with the gallery closed. And I think I'll be ready for some serious escape," she said, hoping she hid the disappointment that swept through her when he gave his departure date.

She was afraid to trust her own feelings in the matter, having so recently been burned by his brother. Were they more alike than she wanted to believe? Was there any truth to Jocelyn's accusations that if Trace tried to make a play it was to one-up his brother?

She didn't think Trace played games like that. But on the day she got engaged, she'd have said the same thing about Tommy.

At six forty-five the next evening, Callie unlocked the doors to the gallery. She and Suzanne both wore black cocktail dresses. Marcie had set up the hors d'oeuvres and wine at a spot near the sales counter. She and another woman would staff it during the evening, keeping everything replenished.

The lighting had come off perfect, highlighting the pictures and drawings to perfection. Callie especially liked how the pen-and-ink drawings looked so dramatic--their stark lines such a contrast from the colorful paintings.

"If no one comes, we'll have enough food to last us for a month," she commented to Suzanne as she straightened the spread of brochures on a small table near the door. Tommy's face smiled up at her.

Callie tried once again to see the differences between the two brothers. Tommy lacked the steadiness Trace evidenced.

She could depend on Trace. If she could get beyond Tommy's betrayal. It wasn't fair to tar Trace with the same brush, just because he looked like his brother.

And because he'd seen that woman in Boston.

"At least he was up-front about it," she said softly.

"What?" Suzanne asked.

"Nothing."

Would he have said anything if his mother hadn't asked?

"Here comes the first customer. Oh, it's Trace. I don't guess he'll be buying anything." Suzanne gave him a wide smile. "Welcome."

Trace had dressed in his business suit for the evening. The snowy-white shirt contrasted with his deep tan. His blue eyes seemed to smile when he spotted Callie.

Casting a curious glance around the gallery, he absorbed everything as he walked over to her.

"It looks terrific. Better than I expected, given what you had to work with."

"There speaks a son of a famous painter. I bet most of the tourists who stop by over the next week will love some of these seascapes," Suzanne said.

"We're hoping for that, anyway. And the publicity of his being a local artist will help," Callie said. She hoped someone would buy one painting. Just one.

The chimes at the door sounded as a couple hesitantly entered.

"I think I'll prop open the door. I don't want there to be any question we're open for business," Callie said.

By seven-thirty the gallery was full of both locals and

tourists. Other gallery owners from nearby towns had stopped by to offer support and see what the work of Jocelyn Warren's son was like. The remarks were kind, but bland. Except for the pen-and-ink drawings. They brought the most excitement to the event.

"Oh, oh, trouble at six o'clock," Trace said softly to Callie. They had just walked away from talking with the mayor of Rocky Point when Trace glanced over her shoulder.

Callie turned and saw Teresa walk into the place as if she were on a mission. She wore skintight black pants and a fuchsia top that hugged her generous endowments. She headed directly to the alcove, scooping up a brochure on her way.

"She has as much right as anyone else to be here. I just hope she doesn't cause trouble," Callie said.

There was no way anyone was going to ignore her. Her hair cascaded halfway down her back. She walked as though she was on a model's runway. Her makeup would keep the cosmetic business in the black for a year. She so didn't look as if she belonged in the gallery.

Trace gave her a disbelieving look. "Honey, women like Teresa *are* trouble. They don't just cause it."

Lord, keep things civil, please. Let this tribute to Tommy go off without a hitch, please. Callie prayed.

Callie watched Teresa for a moment, but she seemed to be doing little more than checking the pricing and noting them on the catalog. There was an order form in the back with the prices listed, but Callie didn't feel the need to inform the woman. Let her figure it out for herself.

Teresa was not high on Callie's list of favorite people.

She couldn't help remembering the shock of finding this woman in bed with her fiancé. Or the disbelief that she'd stood casually wrapped in a sheet and witnessed the scene between Tommy and herself. He could have at least had the decency to tell her to get lost while they were breaking up.

Just then there was an increase in the noise level and she turned, seeing Jocelyn and Montgomery enter like royalty. Locals went to greet them, whether they knew them or not. Both were famous residents and that was enough.

Callie moved through the crowd to greet them. Magically the group around them parted, allowing them a clear path to the alcove.

Jocelyn walked stoically to the exhibit. Her eyes swept the display. She gasped.

"What have you done?" she hissed, staring at the paintings.

Moving closer she looked at the left wall. A half dozen seascapes mingled with some garden studies. She examined each painting, exclaiming with outrage. Moving to the back wall, she let out a low groan.

"How dare you put up sketches! This was not what Tommy was about. He was a gifted painter. Where are his masterpieces? You have ruined everything. I demand you get his better works out here immediately. How dare you make a mockery of all he stood for!"

She turned and saw Teresa. She glared at her. "What are you doing here?"

"I came to see Tommy's paintings," the woman said. "I have every right to be here, maybe more than most. Tommy talked a good line, but he obviously had an inflated opinion of his worth."

Jocelyn turned to Callie. "Is this some kind of retribution for an imagined betrayal because of this floozy? Where are the good paintings? How dare you malign Tommy's memory this way! I trusted you. You of all people should have done your best by him. He loved you. You were to be married. How can you call yourself a respectable gallery dealer when you play such a rotten trick behind my back?"

The crowd fell silent as Jocelyn's voice rose.

"These are his good paintings," Callie said quietly, excruciatingly aware of the silence around them. Every eye was trained on Jocelyn. "His best, actually. I suspected they weren't of the caliber you expected. But they're the best I found. This is why I asked you repeatedly to come see them first. Jocelyn, this is his best work."

"Liar! He had a portfolio from years of work. I should have selected the paintings myself. It was too painful, but this is beyond anything. You've besmirched his good name. How dare you! Take these down immediately. I will not have them up for people to think of as Tommy's work. And I'll see to it that no respectable artist ever deals with you again!"

The crowd seemed to move closer, so not to miss a single nuance of the scene unfolding.

"That's enough, Mother," Trace said, stepping in to grasp her arm. He gently led her through the crowd.

"Do not take that woman's side in this. She's ruined

your brother's reputation. How dare she put up such amateurish paintings! It's to get back at the family because of that woman's allegations she's carrying Tommy's child. It's a lie. How could Callie ever believe such a thing? She was engaged to him! Tommy loved her."

Trace didn't say anything, but relentlessly drew his mother into the privacy of the workshop in the back. Callie almost ran to catch up with them, Montgomery right beside her.

Once inside, Callie wanted to sink through the floor. What must everyone think? It seemed as if a good third of the town was present. Every single person there would have heard every word. Would they think that she'd deliberately put up poor quality work?

What would this do to her gallery's reputation?

She pushed the door, but before it closed, Teresa walked in. She was the one who slammed the door.

"If you want proof this baby is Tommy's, I'll have it soon. My doctor agreed to do the DNA testing," she said.

Callie knew the evening just got worse.

Jocelyn glared at her. "You slut. Stay away from my family. Montgomery, get rid of her."

"Now, my dear, let's hear what she has to say. If DNA testing shows she's carrying our son's baby, maybe we misjudged things." He looked at Teresa expectantly.

"Never. Tommy was engaged to Callie," Jocelyn said, glaring at Teresa.

"Until I found him in bed with Teresa," Callie said. If the damage Jocelyn had done stuck, she could be looking to open a gallery in a new town before long.

"What?" Jocelyn looked stunned. "That's not true!"

"Unfortunately it is," Callie said. "Not a happy memory for me. I thought he really loved me."

"He wanted her to sell his paintings. He wanted to make his mark on the world and take me with him when he moved on. We were going to Paris once he got some money of his own," Teresa said. "Now he's gone. God, what a waste. He was so special. And he loved me!"

"What about Callie?" Montgomery asked bewildered.

Teresa shrugged. "She never told him she wanted to go to Paris."

"They were engaged."

"He was using her to get a showing. Once he made some money, we were taking off," Teresa said with a toss of her head.

"I wondered if he hoped I'd be the ticket for some sales. But, Jocelyn, you've seen his best work. Honestly, I selected the ones I thought showed best. Of everything I've seen, and Trace and I went through everything, his pen-and-ink sketches turn out to be the most unique and marketable. They won't ever rival what you earn for your work, but ought to bring in a respectable amount–especially if there's controlled selling, so we don't flood the market."

"Enough to start a college fund for Tommy's child," Trace said.

Jocelyn drew in a deep breath. "He cannot have fathered a child with that woman."

"Sure he could have. Most likely did," Trace said, grimly.

"It's just like him. Only this time I wasn't around to take the fall."

"That was a misunderstanding," Jocelyn snapped.

"What was?" Teresa asked, wide-eyed.

"It's of no concern to you," Jocelyn said. "Get out."

Teresa frowned at her. "I'm leaving. Too much drama. But my attorney's already talked to Tommy's and before long you'll have to acknowledge I'm carrying his child. I want my share for my baby."

"We will do what's right," Trace said, ignoring his mother's groan of protest.

"Okay, then," Teresa said. She turned and opened the door and made a grand exit.

No one spoke for a long moment.

"You know, if she is carrying Tommy's child, that baby will be your first grandchild," Callie said slowly. "A part of Tommy living on."

Jocelyn turned her gaze to Callie. She didn't move for a moment, then her eyes filled with tears. "Was that really his best work?"

Callie nodded.

"You should have gone over the paintings and chosen the ones you liked, Mom," Trace said gently. "Or decided not to submit them to the general public view."

"They are so amateurish," she said, perplexed. "He had such potential as a child. Such promise."

"But no drive to develop it," Trace said. "You know he liked the easy way out."

"And we made it even easier by funding his lifestyle.

Maybe if he'd had a few setbacks like we overcame at the beginning, he'd have tried harder," Montgomery said slowly. He looked sadly at his wife.

"It was because we had it so hard at first I wanted things to be easier for him," she said.

"People gain strength from adversity," Callie said.

Jocelyn went to Montgomery. "Take me home, please."

As they walked to the door, she looked at Callie. "Take everything down and get rid of it all. I do not want the entire town laughing at Tommy."

"They aren't laughing, Jocelyn. The work shows what Rocky Point is famous for, our coast and seascapes. There'll be people who will enjoy looking at the paintings, not caring whether they are stellar work or not or by some famous artist. The images will bring them pleasure."

Callie's heart ached for the defeated woman. She'd come to terms with Tommy months ago. Jocelyn had to face up to facts now.

Jocelyn just shook her head. "My precious son."

"You have another," Callie said, angry the woman couldn't seem to see beyond her image of one son to the reality of another.

Montgomery looked at Trace. "We do indeed. And a fine man, one I'm proud of."

Trace inclined his head slightly. "Thanks, Dad."

Jocelyn leaned against Montgomery and didn't say a word.

When they had left, Callie leaned against one of the work-tables. "I hate to go back out there," she said, looking at the closed door separating them from the gallery.

"Adversity strengthens you," he murmured. Holding out his hand, he waited.

She put hers into it.

"I hate it when people quote my own words back at me."

He laughed. "You're strong enough. You and your gallery will survive this. Most people will see it as merely an acknowledgment of a man who died young. Sentimentality never hurt artistic sales, you know."

Feeling better about everything with Trace's hand wrapped around hers, she moved to the door. It wasn't fair to leave Suzanne in the lurch.

Head held high, Callie stepped into the gallery. The level of conversation had resumed to its earlier level. It didn't appear as if the crowd had diminished at all. She looked for Suzanne, surprised to see her behind the counter, a line of people clearly waiting to be served.

Her friend Margo came up from behind her.

"Callie, this is fantastic! I hear everyone is hurrying to buy something because Jocelyn Warren told you not to sell anything. Is that true?"

"She said it, but she's not the one in charge," Trace said, stepping beside Callie and looking at Margo.

"Margo, this is Trace Warren."

"I figured that out myself when I saw him. Margo Rogers. I knew you were twins, but you could be Tommy standing here. I'm sure you've heard that a million times."

He inclined his head, his gaze then scanning the room

and the line at the counter.

"Do we tell them the paintings will remain available?" Callie asked doubtfully.

"Are you nuts? This is the best thing to happen," Margo said. "No need to worry about the reputation of your gallery now, Callie. It'll be forever known as a happening place. I'm just sorry I got here too late for the big scene. I can't believe Teresa showed up."

"You know her?" Trace asked.

Margo shook her head. "Only what I've heard from Callie. I didn't know Tommy did pen-and-ink drawings. They're really good. If he did some of the cove, I might be interested in one myself."

"I knew he sketched sometimes, but I had no idea of the number of pieces he'd done. I expect Trace'll be able to sell them a few at a time for years to come. And their value will only increase since no more will be forthcoming," Callie said, breathing a little more easily that the mood of the event seemed to have moved to upbeat and positive.

"I'm going to mingle and scoop up any gossip I can," Margo said with a wide smile. She sauntered back toward the alcove, stopping to speak to a couple she knew.

"It seems a long time until nine," Callie said, glancing at her watch. "I'll go help Suzanne."

Chapter Sixteen

Trace tried to stay in the background, but once alone, it was as if he were fair game. Men and women who'd known Tommy came over to talk to him. Many asked if he, too, was artistic. They seemed surprised when he told them he was an engineer.

More than one woman flirted. He wasn't surprised. People often confused him and Tommy when his brother had been alive. For the first time since arriving, he couldn't wait to return to the Amazon. At least there he knew what to expect.

By nine, he was happier than Callie to close the gallery. There were people lingering, still talking, eating the delicious hors d'oeuvres and getting one last glass of wine. He wanted to suggest they take it with them, but knew that wouldn't go over big.

He looked for Callie, seeing her with a customer, laughing at something the woman had said. How she could still look fresh and happy was beyond him. He knew she'd had a long day. The dramatic scene with his mother couldn't have helped. Yet to look at her, she looked as if she didn't have a care in the world.

Finally the last of the guests left. Callie closed the door and pulled the shade, leaning against the wooden frame.

"I'm beat!" she said.

"Me, too," Suzanne said, kicking off her high heels.

"Me, too," Marcie said, as she and her assistant began to competently package up the leftover food. "Want this now, or shall I freeze it?" she asked.

"Leave enough for me and Suzanne for a couple of days now and freeze the rest. Thanks again, Marcie, it was lovely as always."

"I'll say," Suzanne said, coming to the counter and swiping another canape.

"If I hadn't been so busy, I'd have eaten more, but I had my hands full. We sold everything and have several wanting to see what else is available. I have a list."

She grabbed a couple more crab puffs before Marcie wrapped them up.

"Fantastic. Let's deliver all the sold items and showcase other paintings and see if we can sell some of those, as well this next week," Callie said, pushing away and walking to the alcove.

"In addition, several of the people also bought the frames the paintings are in, so I'll need to get some replacements. Same with the pen-and-ink frames. I think I'll plan to sell those in the frames from now on."

She walked around the display, already deep in thought. Trace wondered if she remembered the rest of them were there.

"Come by tomorrow and we'll pick out some more. Or I

can bring all I have here and you can sell them as you can. Unless you don't have the room," he said.

She turned and frowned.

"That'd put me short on storage space, but when you leave, I'll need access. Let me rearrange some things in back and see if we can squeeze them in."

Trace waited until Callie was ready to leave before saying, "I want to take you home. It's late."

"My car's here. I wasn't planning to walk home this late."

"It'll be safe here overnight."

She nodded. Bidding Suzanne good-night once she left Callie locked up and went with Trace to his rental car.

"Are you holding up all right?" he asked as he drove the short distance to her flat.

She nodded. Truth be told, she was more worried about Trace and his relationship with his parents than the situation with Tommy.

She'd had several months to get over the initial hurt and betrayal. But Trace and Jocelyn and Montgomery had only learned the facts recently.

He walked her up to her flat, stopping at the door. Taking her key he unlocked it for her.

"Did you want to come in?" she asked breathlessly.

"Not tonight. I'll have the paintings ready to go in the morning. Take care of yourself," he said, brushing his lips lightly over hers.

Turning to leave, Trace regretted not staying. But Callie was tired.

Plus, he didn't want sympathy tonight. If she was only feeling sorry for the family because of the revelations from Teresa, he'd just as soon not know that.

He was not after his brother's fiance. Now that he knew Callie had ended that relationship before his death, weren't all bets off? She was not Tommy's fiancé.

And Trace was growing more and more interested in the gallery owner than might be good for either of them.

The next morning Callie felt better about things. She rose early and quickly dressed in jeans and a loose top. She'd get the paintings and pen-and-ink drawings from Trace and find room for them in her workshop area. Suzanne could hold the fort for a while. Once back at the gallery, Callie'd have to work quickly to get another batch of paintings ready for sale. She was delighted the pictures had sold and hoped many more would find buyers.

Stopping at Marcie's, she was surprised to find her friend already behind the counter.

"Don't you ever rest?" Callie asked with a wide smile.

"I could ask the same thing. What can I get you?"

"Breakfast for two again? I should've called, but this is a spur-of-the-moment decision. I'll have a cup of coffee while I wait."

By the time she turned on the road that led to the cottage, Callie felt like a teenage girl going on a first date. She could hardly wait to see Trace again. The burden of the opening night had lifted. The exhibit was going to be a success.

Jocelyn had seen the worst and dealt with it. Learned the

truth and was going to have to find her own way to deal with that.

Now Callie wished she was strong enough to trust her instincts. She was uncertain about any future with Trace Warren, but for once was going to quell those doubts and see what unfolded. *Trust in the Lord, always,* she murmured under her breath.

She had to park on the street as there was another car in the driveway beside Trace's. Callie didn't recognize it as one of the Warrens' vehicles. For a moment, she stayed in her car, indecision causing her to consider returning home and eating two breakfasts.

But it could be anyone, the cottage owner, a Realtor. Maybe she should find out who.

Anyway, she and Trace had agreed upon nine this morning and it was already ten after. He was expecting her.

She lifted the basket Marcie had prepared and headed for the front door. It was wide-open.

"Trace?" she called.

There was no response.

He wouldn't leave with the door open if he was going anywhere. Plus his rental car was in the driveway.

Callie stepped inside.

She put the basket down on the table near the sofa and headed for the studio. Maybe he'd started packing up the paintings.

As she neared the door, she could hear the murmur of voices, then silence.

She stepped into the room, stopping in shock. Teresa

had her arms around Trace's neck. They were kissing.

Deja vu. She saw Tommy and Teresa. Now Trace and Teresa.

Had their mother been right–what Tommy had, Trace wanted?

For a moment she was frozen in place. The past could not be repeating itself. It wasn't fair!

She must have made a sound because Trace's hands came up and pulled Teresa's arms down, stepping away and turning to look at Callie.

Less than a second had passed, yet she felt as if the world slowed.

"Sorry. Guess I got my wires crossed," she said, spinning around and almost running out of the cottage.

"Callie, wait," he called behind her.

She could hear Teresa say something, but not make out the words.

She didn't care. She just wanted to get away from the cottage and never return. It was definitely jinxed!

She opened the car door, but before it moved six inches, Trace slammed it shut, leaning against it. "You need to listen to me. It is not what it looked like."

"It looked like two people kissing. What part of that isn't what it looks like?" she snapped.

She refused to look at him. He was as big a betrayer as his brother. Why had she fooled herself that they could be different?

"She was kissing me," he said.

"Oh, I see, slender female overpowering muscular male.

Yep, I get that picture. Not."

He put the edge of his hand beneath her chin and raised her face until her gaze met his.

"I was not kissing Teresa. She kissed me. She arrived at nine. I thought it was you when she knocked. I think she figures one brother is as good as the other."

Callie stared at him. Was he serious? Or was he trying to put an acceptable spin on things?

"Callie, there's nothing between me and Teresa," he repeated.

"I do not think of you as Tommy," she repeated. "Yet you don't believe that. So why should I believe you?"

Trace dropped his hand and stepped back, his eyes narrowed as he regarded her for a long moment. "Impasse."

He glanced over at the cottage. Callie looked, as well, and saw Teresa standing in the doorway. She sashayed down, her expression of satisfaction clear for all to see.

"See you later," she said, waving several fingers at Trace. With a smirk at Callie, she went to her car and got inside.

"Blast it!" Trace slammed a fist against the top of Callie's car. "I told you she was pure trouble."

Callie watched as Teresa backed out. For a moment she felt a stab of hurt, then the smug look on the woman's face got to her. Was she deliberately causing trouble?

"Why?" Callie asked, turning back to look at Trace.

"You heard her. She said I really reminded her of Tommy. One guy's as good as the next for her, I guess. Anyway, we could keep it all in the family, with her carrying my brother's baby and all. Since we're twins, we have the same DNA, so it would be like having the child's father."

Callie couldn't believe it. "Is she nuts?"

For a moment Trace held his breath. "I think so. Or mercenary. She has a better shot at the Warren money if there's more than the baby involved."

He watched Callie as she thought through the situation. He couldn't believe Teresa had come on to him like that. If she'd loved his brother, as she claimed, he was not some stand-in.

But it wasn't Teresa and his brother he was concerned about. It was this woman standing here. He knew Tommy had given her a rough time. Could she ever look at him and not see his twin? Ever look at him and see commitment and fidelity and not betrayal. How that scene must have replayed in her mind and seeing Teresa with him had to cause her pain all over again.

Without giving him a clue what she was thinking, she took her hand away from the door handle and turned toward the cottage.

"I brought breakfast. I didn't know if you'd had yours yet. It's probably cold by now. But I'm hungry. Then I need to get the paintings ready for pickup. Margo's friend Mike is supposed to be here this morning to transport them for me."

"I haven't had breakfast. And after the dramatics, I could use something. Did you bring any coffee?" Trace asked, walking with her up the walkway.

Did she believe him or not?

He'd known Teresa's type the moment he saw her. She was so like Gwen in college. Tommy always ran true to form.

"I brought everything," she said.

She handed him the basket when he followed her into the cottage. He took it to the dining nook and opened it up. The carafe kept the coffee hot. The warming tray kept the food warm. This was the second time Callie had brought him breakfast. The first he understood--damage control. But why this morning?

She went to the kitchen and got out plates and eating utensils. In only a moment she set the table and sat in one of the chairs. The one she always used when she came before?

He didn't like the thought of her knowing more about the cottage than he did.

It wasn't something he'd admit to a living soul, but he was jealous of his brother and the relationship he had at one time with this woman. Trace wanted her to look at him with interest. With love.

Trace watched Callie as she began to eat. He took a bite. The omelet was light and fluffy and full of ham, cheese, mushrooms and scallions. A man could forget about working in the Amazon Basin if he had meals like this every day.

"About Teresa," he began.

"No," Callie said. "You"ll understand if I don't wish to discuss the woman. I can't think of a single happy memory involving her."

"As long as you understand she was kissing me, not vice versa."

Callie inclined her head, concentrating on her breakfast.

Trace grew frustrated. He wanted her to say she believed him. That she knew he'd never be interested in anyone like

Teresa.

"She's not my type," he almost growled.

She looked up at that. "You have a type?"

He'd just made things worse.

"No. I mean nothing about her appeals to me."

"It sure did to your brother."

"We are not alike for all we looked similar."

"Mmm," she said, reaching for the carafe of coffee and pouring herself a cup.

"And that means?"

"Trace, I know you and your brother are nothing alike. He was charming and knew how to sweep a woman off her feet. But he had no substance. Much as I thought I was in love with him, I must have known deep inside that it wouldn't work. We never set a wedding date."

Trace didn't know how to take that bit of information. He almost winced when she said they were nothing alike and Tommy had been charming. So he wasn't charming. He'd known that all his life. He liked her comment about substance. She must think he had it if she continued the comparison.

Did that mean she didn't see him as a stand-in for his brother?

Yet when he'd kissed her, she'd called Tommy's name.

She studied him for a moment. Trace caught her gaze and regarded her with every appearance of confidence. But he wondered what she was thinking.

"You're planning to leave at the end of next week, right?" she said.

"Next Friday."

Once the paintings were in her gallery and he finished sorting through Tommy's papers, there'd be nothing holding him here.

And the bridge wasn't going to build itself.

"How about we make a pact. I'll show you around Rocky Point and the area, we'll make some memories together and neither one of us will ever mention Tommy or Teresa the entire week."

That floored him. After all she'd witnessed today, she wanted to make memories together?

"Why?" he asked warily.

"Why not?" she countered.

"I can think of a couple of reasons. Humor me."

"Your career takes you far from this area. Who knows when you'll be back this way. I'd love for you to remember me when you're in the Amazon Basin, or bridging some raging river in Africa. And I still want those photographs. I was serious about that."

"Is this the gallery owner offering to keep a potential artist happy?" he asked.

She shrugged. "We could look at it that way if you want."

It was not the way he wanted to look at it. But it'd give him six days with her without dealing with the ghost of Tommy between them.

In that time surely he'd know if he could ever get past that ghost to form a lasting relationship with this woman.

Teresa wasn't his type, but Callie could be.

"What do you have in mind?" he asked.

"I have to work today. Any chance you want to help me select the next batch of paintings to display?"

"I suggest you let my mother do that. I think it'd help her to get involved."

Callie nodded. "Good idea. I'll call her as soon as I get to the gallery."

"No need. I have her number programmed into my cell phone."

He withdrew it from his pocket and hit the speed dial number.

"Hello?" Jocelyn answered.

"Mom? Trace here. Callie and I are having breakfast and she wanted to know if you'd help select the next batch of paintings for display."

"What are you talking about?" Jocelyn asked.

"The paintings on display last night were sold out. Callie wants to show some others and see if those would also sell."

"The paintings sold?" Jocelyn asked.

"They're not up to your standards, but they weren't totally horrible," Trace said.

"Why are you and Callie having breakfast together?"

It was the opening he'd been hoping for. "We're seeing each other."

Callie dropped her fork and stared at him. Trace winked.

"I'll think about it," Jocelyn said, and hung up.

"What're you thinking? You can't tell your mother something like that!" Callie said, glaring at him.

"Why not, I'm looking at you and seeing you, you're

looking at me and seeing me. So we're seeing each other."

"You know what she'll think."

"So what?" he challenged.

"So--" She stopped and looked puzzled. "So I guess we just agreed to do that very thing."

Trace nodded in satisfaction. He was looking forward to the next six days.

By mid afternoon all the paintings had been moved from the cottage and placed in the gallery's workshop. Callie had copies of the appraisals made to keep in the gallery, as well as the formal report she'd given Trace.

He'd helped until a few minutes ago, then disappeared.

"We can hardly turn around in here," Suzanne commented. She'd kept the gallery going while Callie had been moving the canvasses. Now she came into the workshop area to see what they had.

"I've had lots of requests today for more of these seascapes. Are we going to frame them first?" she said.

"We probably ought to offer the option. I hope I have enough frames. The exhibit's only for a few days. Any leftover inventory can then get framed later."

"Did I tell you two women today asked where they could contribute to the baby fund? They didn't want to ask you, being sure you'd be too devastated to respond. But they heard about our fun and games of last night and wanted to help the poor new mother," Suzanne said warily, as if afraid of Callie's response.

"You're making that up," Callie said with a small laugh.

Suzanne shook her head. "No. I knew you'd be floored.

Can you imagine anyone less in need of help than Teresa? Good grief, most of the men here had to wipe the drool from their chins when she walked out. She'll be just fine."

"She was trying for Trace this morning," Callie said.

"Now you're making that up," Suzanne said with a broad smile.

"Nope, walked in on a lip-lock that didn't quit."

Suzanne's amusement fled. "Are you sure he was a willing partner?"

"He said not."

"And you believe him? After Tommy, I'd suspect anyone in that family."

Callie nodded. "I have to believe him. I want him to believe me when I tell him something. I need to learn to trust unless I find out trust isn't warranted."

Instinctively she knew Trace was someone to depend upon. But her heart had a hard time believing that.

"I know he's yummy and all. And really more of a man if you know what I mean than his brother. But you're not falling for him are you?" Suzanne asked with concern.

"Not really falling. Just—interested?"

"Because he looks like Tommy?"

"I guess everyone thinks that. He's his own unique person. One I'm more attracted to than I was to Tommy. He's leaving soon and I may never see him again. I want the next few days to be perfect."

"What's happening the next few days?"

"I'm showing him around Rocky Point."

"To make him fall in love with you?" Suzanne guessed.

Callie stared at her. Put that way, it was stupid beyond belief.

"You're right. How dumb can one person be?" she asked.

"Hey, I didn't say anything about being dumb. Just think a minute. He doesn't live here. He's working in Brazil. Do you know how far away that is? You can't open a gallery there. What are you going to do, see him Christmas and vacations? You're coming off a bad experience with Tommy. Don't ricochet to some other guy so soon. Take your time and find the right one."

Callie nodded, turning away.

She was afraid Trace was the right one. Tommy had been the warm-up, Trace was the real thing.

What was she going to do? She couldn't pack up and move, even if Trace asked her. Her life was here, and his wasn't.

Even if he felt the same way about her, she didn't see a future together. There was too much between them. Not the least of which was Tommy Warren.

Chapter Seventeen

Monday morning dawned with scattered clouds. Callie dressed in shorts and a pullover cotton top, kept an eye on the sky. She and Trace were going sailing today, unless the weather made it impossible. She didn't take chances. If there was a storm brewing, they'd stay on shore.

But a few puffy clouds didn't necessarily mean a storm. She finished dressing and hurried into the kitchen to turn on the radio. The news was on. She half listened as she prepared breakfast, waiting for the weather. Finally the forecast. Scattered showers, possibility of thundershowers in late afternoon.

She went to the window and scanned the sky. They could have a short sail and return before the thunderstorms blew up. She really didn't want to miss going out with him today. Their time together was rapidly drawing to a close.

Callie called Trace at seven-thirty.

"Warren," he answered.

"Are you still game? They're predicting scattered showers this afternoon, but so far there's more blue in the sky than clouds."

"You're the captain, you call the shots."

Callie appreciated his vote of confidence. "Then I say we head out. If it starts to look threatening, we'll return to port."

"I'll meet you at the dock at eight," Trace said.

Callie was already on the boat when Trace arrived. She had everything packed away for lunch.

"Permission to come aboard, Captain?" Trace called from the dock.

"Permission granted," she said with a bright smile.

When he stepped onboard, she reached up and gave him a kiss of welcome. She stepped back but he caught her around the waist and held her against him.

"Nice welcome, but you can do better than that," he said, lowering his mouth to hers and giving her a kiss that melted her knees.

A whistle from one of the other boaters in the marina broke them apart.

"Great, there goes my reputation," she murmured, laughing as she looked around to find the culprit.

"Or enhances it. What can I do?" Trace asked.

"Not a thing until we clear the marina. Then we'll hoist the sails and fly before the wind," she said, already blowing the engine compartment in preparation for starting the motor.

They had to watch out for the myriad of other boats already on the bay. Callie was a bit surprised to find so many boats on a Monday, but it was the height of the summer season and tourists and visitors abounded. She skillfully handled the boat and soon left the more crowded waters behind. The sun played peekaboo behind clouds. When shining it was hot.

"Know any places to swim?" Trace asked, sitting beside her and casually putting his arm around her shoulders.

"There're some more isolated beaches around the headland. The water's pretty cold."

"I remember from summers I spent here. But I came prepared in case we can swim."

"I have a swimsuit onboard. Sometimes the temperature climbs too high not to indulge," she said. "Want a turn steering?"

"Sure."

They changed places and she gave him a couple of pointers. He held the boat at the right angle to reap full benefit of the wind. They skimmed across the water, encountering only the mildest of swells. Clouds continued to gather overhead.

Callie took charge again when they approached the beach she wanted, though she felt Trace probably could have managed without any help from her. She headed for the one spot on the shore where she could get the boat in close. In no time they were anchored within a few yards of a sheltered beach. The water lapped the sandy shore. Trees growing near the sand gave wide swaths of shade.

"We can swim and then eat," she suggested.

Trace agreed. He wore his swimsuit beneath his khakis.

Callie had to change. She went to the small cabin and soon had on her swimsuit. Somehow it had not seemed so skimpy when she was swimming with Margo. She took a breath and flung open the door to step out on the deck.

Trace turned and let his gaze sweep over her his smile showing appreciation.

"I could use some sun screen," she said, offering the bottle of lotion. "If you could get my back, I can do the rest."

He took the bottle and poured the lotion in his palm, motioning for her to turn around. Callie had been trying to ignore the expanse of tanned chest inches away. Her fingers actually tingled in longing to rub against that warm skin. She longed to lean closer and breathe in his scent.

She turned and closed her eyes. They were going swimming, nothing more. They were seeing if they could become friends. That was a long way from what she wanted at this moment. Could they skip the preliminaries and get right down to it?

The lotion was cool against her skin, but his warm hand soon changed that. He carefully spread it over her shoulders, down her back, slipping beneath the narrow band of her bathing suit top to cover her skin. Lower, down her back to the edge of the pants of the suit. Her heart raced. Her breathing seemed constricted. She needed to jump into that icy water right away!

"Now you can return the favor," he said holding out the bottle.

She opened her eyes and turned, reaching for the suntan lotion. She poured some into her palm, put the bottle down and rubbed her hands together. He'd already turned, presenting that muscular back that was as tanned as any she'd seen.

"Doesn't look like you need it. Do you work without a shirt in the Amazon?"

"Sometimes. It's so humid there clothing sticks. I always wear sun screen."

It was pure delight touching him. She ran her hands over his back, feeling the strength of the muscles, the heat of his skin. He was rock-solid. She brushed the hair at his neck, making sure she covered every inch of skin. He felt so good. His back tapered toward his waist. She noted the difference in breadth as she ran her hands down along his spine, out around toward his ribs, back up across his shoulder blade.

"All done," she tried to say brightly. Only her voice sounded husky and low.

Trace turned and looked at her. She met his gaze, knowing he'd see the awareness she couldn't hide.

He slowly reached out and drew her into his arms, pressing her closer as he began to kiss her. His mouth moved against hers, demanding a response she was only too willing to give. His hand moved across her back.

Callie gave a sigh of pleasure.

She loved this man.

Dare she take such a chance again?

Only, what choice did she have. Her heart was taken. The question now was what to do about that?

Slowly Trace ended the kiss finally resting his forehead against hers, looking into her eyes. "How far do you want to take this?"

She swallowed. All the way hovered on her lips, but she knew she would be rushing things. She wanted more than just an afternoon together.

"We should stop now," she suggested.

"Then let's go swimming," he said, turning to vault over the side of the boat.

His actions caught her by surprise. She rushed to the side to see him swimming toward the beach. She had to lower the ladder first so they could get back onboard, then finished putting the sun screen on her arms and legs, all the while trying to get some control over her feelings. That kiss had been mind-blowing. She wouldn't mind another few thousands.

Finally she climbed down the ladder until she touched the water, jumping the rest of the way. The shock of cold took her breath away. She came to the surface and began to swim toward Trace. When a cloud blocked the sun, the water turned grey and felt even colder. She was glad to reach the shallows, it was definitely warmer.

"This is great. I can't believe you knew a spot where there aren't a hundred tourists," he said, splashing toward her in the shallows.

She stood up and waded the rest of the way.

"Sometimes there are families here, but more often than not it's deserted. Margo found it first. We love to come here to sunbathe and swim and talk. If you climb the dunes, you'll see the forest comes right to the edge of the water on the other side."

They explored the small beach, then swam some more in the shallows where the water was warmer. The sun continued to appear and disappear. Trace stood and studied the sky at one point. Callie turned and saw the growing bank of dark clouds.

"I suggest we head back for the boat," she said. "Lunch and then we head for home. I don't like sailing in storms-- the wind and water are too unpredictable."

"Good idea. Race you."

Without waiting for her agreement, he plunged into the water. She followed instantly, but knew long before she reached the boat that he could swim faster than she could.

As soon as they got onboard, Callie showed him the small shower to rinse off the salt water, then they dressed.

She brought out lunch and they ate on the bow, facing into the breeze and enjoying the rocking motion.

"A man could get used to this," Trace said, his eyes on the far horizon.

"One day I'd like to get a huge boat, and sail around America. There's so much to see from the Inland Passage to the Inter-coastal waterways. I think it would be great fun. Not that I see myself affording the boat or the time anytime soon. I'll probably have to wait until I'm too old to do it."

"Make plans to do it before you're too old. None of us know how long we'll be here. Don't wait too long," Trace said somberly.

"What is it you'd like to do that you've put off?" she asked.

He was quiet for a long moment.

"Have a family, I guess. In the back of my mind was the thought that someday I'd get married, have some kids, a dog. There'd be family gatherings where there's a lot of laughter and happiness. I missed that growing up. My parents were focused on their work. They shouldn't have had kids. They did their best, but I'd want my family to be different."

Callie was intrigued to find out he wanted a family. Somehow, given his work, she never suspected that.

"Would you expect your family to travel with you or would you find a job closer to home?"

"There're plenty of jobs closer to home. I think a family should stick together, don't you?"

She nodded. "My family's close, except that my parents and grandparents live in Iowa and don't know why I love the sea so much. They come to visit once a year and I go home for Christmas every year. I wouldn't trade anything about my childhood, except maybe to have a brother or sister."

"That can be overrated. Look at the situation with my brother."

"You must have had fun as children," she said.

He shrugged. "When we were young. But from the time we were teenagers, Tommy began pushing the limits. Always looking for an angle, a way to get around rules and regulations. And always after the girls."

"You mentioned when you first met Teresa that this wasn't the first time. Did he get someone else pregnant before?" Callie asked. She'd wondered ever since Trace made that comment.

He nodded.

"Tell me," she said softly.

"We were almost finished our first year of college. He was in danger of being kicked out because of bad grades.

He'd much rather party than study. And his idea of partying was seeing several different girls all at once. Sometimes as Tommy, sometimes as me."

"What?"

"A favorite pastime of his, fool people into thinking he was me."

"So what happened?"

"He got a girl pregnant, only he'd told her he was Trace Warren. She came after me. She swore I was the one. I swore I had never met her before the day she and one of the assistant deans showed up at my dorm room. Tommy offered no help, blandly pretending he hadn't a clue what was going on. But the amusement he couldn't hide made me blow my temper."

"So did he fess up?"

"Only when one of my friends pointed out on several occasions the woman said she was with me, she was not because I was with Jim."

Trace pointed to the area just beneath his left ear. "See this scar?"

She peered at it, a faint line about an inch long. "Yes."

"That's how Jim could tell Tommy and me apart. And he swore I was with him at soccer games when the alleged trysts took place. I think if Jim hadn't stood up for me, I would have been nailed as the father. Tommy fought, but lost. He ended up paying for the child's delivery expenses. The baby was given up for adoption."

"That's why you don't think he would have done right by Teresa," she said slowly.

"Not unless it suited him. Tommy didn't have a very high sense of responsibility."

Callie gathered up the remnants of the meal and put them away in the bag she'd brought, then reached out and took Trace's hand, threading her fingers through his.

"I'm glad you stayed," she said, leaning against his shoulder and gazing out across the sea.

Trace would have sat like this for the rest of the day. Her hand was small in his, held loosely. Her weight leaning against his shoulder was a light pressure he could get used to.

What would it be like to live in a locale like this, to be able to take off sailing whenever time permitted? He'd have to rediscover how to relax. Most of his last few years were spent at job sites where the downtime didn't take a different turn from working.

"Much as I like this, we need to head back," Callie said, raising her head and frowning at the bank of dark clouds in the west.

"You fixed lunch, I'll take us to dinner. How about the Pelican again?"

"Sounds great."

She smiled at him and it was all he could do to stop himself from sweeping her into his arms and taking up where they'd left off earlier.

Before they reached the marina, the rain began. It wasn't a bad storm as Trace thought of one at sea, with high winds and waves braking over the bow, just a steady drizzle of rain, soaking everything.

"Anything I can do?" he asked, standing beside her.

"Sorry about this, I thought we'd beat it back," she said.

"Hey, it's not like we didn't get wet swimming."

"But that was more fun than standing here getting soaked. Aren't you cold?"

She'd donned her clothes and an old windbreaker she'd had in the cabin. She offered him one that belonged to Margo, but he doubted it would fit.

"I'm not cold," he said.

The rain was cool but after the months of heat in the Amazon, he reveled in it. If he got cold, he'd have to see about that jacket, but for now he felt exhilarated.

When they finally docked, Callie apologized again. He stopped her with a kiss.

"It was not dangerous. A little rain never hurt anyone. Stop apologizing."

"I wanted the day to be perfect."

"It was perfect."

"But the rain—"

He put his finger on her lips. "The weather wasn't perfect, but the day's experience was. I had fun, I think you did, as well. Isn't that what we wanted?"

She nodded.

"To build memories together," he said softly.

She seemed startled. Didn't she think he'd remember?

"For us they'll forever be special."

She gave a shy smile. Thanking the Lord for this special man.

"I'll pick you up at seven," he said, brushing his lips against hers again.

They walked back to their cars together and Trace watched as she drove off.

Another of their days together was almost gone. They had three more. Then he'd return to the Amazon Basin and work. And Callie would continue her life here in Rocky Point.

Trace was already wondering if he could swing a trip home at Christmas as he turned into the driveway of the cottage. Was he getting ahead of himself? Or just planning for the future?

His father sat on the porch. Trace was surprised to see him.

"Got caught in the rain?" Montgomery asked as Trace walked up in his wet clothes.

"I sure did. Come in. I'll change and be right with you."

"I'll fix something to drink," Montgomery said, heading for the kitchen.

Trace joined him a few minutes later, dry and warmer.

"I didn't expect you. I was sailing with Callie," Trace said when he entered the kitchen.

"She's pretty, isn't she? Sweet, too. Too good for Tommy. I never thought it'd last. She wasn't bimbo enough for him."

Trace nodded. That described Tommy's girlfriends. He was surprised his father knew that.

"I came to see the pictures," Montgomery said.

Nothing was further from Trace's mind. He stared at his father for a long moment. "You did?"

"Callie had the right of it. We have a son we love. We

need to learn more about him now that he's a man. Tell me about your work."

Chapter Eighteen

Trace knocked on Callie's door at seven. She opened it smiling at him.

"You are always on time. I like that," she said. "I'm ready."

"And I like that, no waiting around while you finish dressing."

She laughed and pulled her door closed. "I know, isn't that the dumbest thing. Where did that come from? I think punctuality is not rated high enough. You get dried out after the rain?"

"My father was at the cottage when I got there. He came to see my photographs. He only left a little while ago. It surprised me to see him."

"Why? I'd think a parent would want to know about his child and what he was doing."

"First time."

"So, better than no time. Did he like them?"

"From an artistic point of view?"

"No, from learning more about what you do," she said as he opened the car door for her.

"He had lots of questions. I think he left knowing more

what I do and why."

"That's what parents should do."

"Do yours?"

"Heavens, yes. My mother is always giving me advice on how to better display paintings when I send her pictures of the displays. Or which carpeting to get next. Dad offered to help make me a balcony garden if I wanted to grow my own vegetables. He can't understand not wanting to grow things."

"Did they meet Tommy?"

She shook her head.

"Why not?"

"They're coming out in a couple of weeks. At the time I got engaged, I thought there was no rush. Then later, I was glad they hadn't."

Trace wondered what Callie's parents were like. He'd heard meeting a person's parents could give someone an idea of what that person would be like in thirty years. He hoped that wasn't strictly true. He didn't want to be like either of his parents, now or in the future.

"I hope you're planning on dancing," Callie said. "I wore my dancing shoes."

"Why else go to the Pelican?" he responded.

Forget thinking about parents. Tonight was for the two of them.

The days flew by. Tuesday Callie took off from work and they went clamming--ending up with a group of her friends at a big clambake on the beach. Only one or two people mistakenly called Trace Tommy. The rest welcomed him for who he was and had no trouble keeping his identity straight.

Wednesday Callie and Trace drove to Portland and went antique shopping. She was looking for some old display cases to incorporate in her gallery, but found nothing she wanted. Still, the time together was what counted. And Trace was as interested in the history of some of the antique pieces of furniture as she was.

Thursday she had to meet with some artists and a serious collector. Once work was finished, they caught a matinee at the local theater, enjoying a romantic comedy together.

That night they ate dinner at her flat.

Callie set the table with candles, her best china and silverware. The wineglasses sparkled in the flickering light. The rest of the apartment shone. She'd made sure his last evening would be special. For dinner she was having clam chowder, lobster and crusty French bread. His mother hadn't provided his favorite meal, but Callie would.

Nothing had been said about the future. Would he bid her farewell tonight and head back to work and forget about her within the week?

"Maybe not that soon, but will he come back to see me? Somehow discover he can't live without me?" she said aloud, already feeling blue that he was going.

Lord let tonight be a happy one, I trust in you to take care of the future, she mumbled as she put finishing touches on a small flower arrangement.

When everything was ready, she sank on the sofa and gazed out the window. Rain was again predicted. They couldn't even take a last walk around town. After dinner, he'd thank her for the meal and leave. Return to the Inn where he'd moved yesterday after winding up the last of Tommy's affairs and closing the cottage. It would be rented to someone else within days. Summer demand was always high.

Callie wasn't sorry to know she'd never go there again. But she didn't like the finality of everything.

He knocked, right at seven. She could set her watch by him.

She rose and crossed to the door, smiling for joy at seeing him. Hoping the sadness that threatened to overwhelm her would remain at bay until he left tonight.

"For you," Trace said, flourishing a bouquet of colorful flowers. Their fragrance filled the entryway.

"They're beautiful."

She swallowed hard, blinking to keep the tears at bay. She hadn't been given flowers many times in her life. How sweet he'd give her some today. A farewell gift. She refused to think about it.

"Let me get them in some water."

He followed her into the kitchen area as she found a vase and filled it with water. The arrangement was lovely. She placed them in the center of the table, moving the arrangement she'd put there.

He came over and drew her into his arms, kissing her gently.

"I have your favorite dinner," she said a minute later, pushing away lest she grab hold and never let go.

"You cooked lobster?"

She laughed. "Once again Marcie to the rescue. She prepared everything. I have it all warming. I wanted your last night here to be special."

"Do you like lobster?" he asked.

"I love it. But I don't cook it. Too traumatic."

He smiled at the face she made.

Plunging live lobsters into boiling water was not her idea of cooking. She much preferred Marcie do the awful deed. Callie liked to think her lobster came from the supermarket neatly wrapped in cellophane, not live from the sea.

"Are you all set to leave?" she asked once they were seated at the table with their dinner in front of them, hoping her voice didn't betray her sadness.

"Packed and ready. I'll have to go early in the morning to get to Logan Airport in time for the flight. I'll turn in the rental car there," Trace said calmly.

The least he could do was look regretful or somehow sad, she thought, feeling the minutes fly by. Only a couple of hours and she'd have to say goodbye.

She wasn't ready.

For a moment her throat closed up. There was so much more to say, but she felt tongue-tied.

"This is delicious," Trace said as he ate the chowder. "Rich and flavorful."

"Marcie's a great cook. Sadly I'm not. It's not worth it to cook much for one. When I have friends over, we usually all bring something, more like a potluck. I eat out a lot."

She was babbling. She'd already told him that earlier in their relationship.

"At least you have the choice. For us it's the company's chow line or nothing," Trace said.

"I guess you make up for it when you hit a city."

"First stop is always a fine restaurant. Or the bar, for some guys."

"You're excited to be going back, aren't you?"

"I've missed several weeks. Never been away in the middle of a job like that before."

"Will you take time off at Christmas?"

He was silent for a moment, studying her.

"Will you be here at Christmas?" he asked.

"Probably Iowa."

Should she invite him there?

"We're sure to have snow. Want to come?"

He shook his head. "With any luck we'll be in the final stages of construction. That's summer there and we work long hours while daylight is plentiful."

"What about Tommy's estate?"

"I think I've got everything lined up. The attorney knows what I want. It's just a question of winding up the legal work. If the DNA test shows Teresa's baby is Tommy's, and I believe her, I'll set up a trust for the child. I'm not giving the money to her, but will put my father and the attorney as trustees to see to the baby's welfare. I've given the attorney my phone and e-mail address, so he can contact me if anything else comes up. And he said he'll fax any paperwork I need to sign. And he knows it might be some time before I respond. Which reminds me."

He reached into his pocket and pulled out a card, putting

it on the table near Callie.

"Contact information. In case you want to write or something."

She reached for the card, a broad smile plastered on her face. She was fighting tears.

In case she wanted to? Try and stop her. If that's all they had for the foreseeable future, she'd make the most of it.

"I'm taking one of the programs from the gallery back with me, it has your e-mail address on it," he said.

"You'll be going back to winter," she said.

"Winter in the Amazon isn't much different from summer, except for shorter days. Still hot and humid. Will you write?"

She nodded, blinking to keep the tears at bay. "Of course. I'll let you know how the sketches sell, and what your mother is doing and—"

"Mostly I want to know what you're doing," he interjected.

"I'll be working at the gallery."

"And sailing, going to clambakes. Discovering new talent. I want to hear it all."

"You do?" It was a very routine life she led. She was surprised he wanted to know everything.

"I like this slice of life you have for yourself, Callie. When I'm lying on my bunk sweltering in the heat, I can read about your sailing in the cool Atlantic. Or up to your knees in the surf digging clams."

"So you'll need to write me about how the bridge is going. And send me pictures. I'll get them printed and see what sells."

They discussed options for Callie's branching out into a different facet of art with photographs. She considered opening a satellite gallery with a separate name, which would offer art more suited to tourists. The more she thought about it, the more excited she became.

She needed to focus on something or her heart would break with Trace's leaving.

She broached the idea to Trace and was surprised to get his wholehearted approval. They discussed the ramifications, where she should locate the shop, start-up costs and other aspects. Before she knew it the meal was over.

It was growing late–it was already dark outside.

She wasn't ready. Why couldn't she make time stand still!

"Thanks for the dinner, it was delicious," Trace said when he finished the last of the chocolate pie.

He put his napkin on the table and pushed back his chair. "I need to get going. I have to get up early for my flight."

She nodded. After all, what was left to say?

Callie walked him to the door. He turned and took her into his arms, kissing her gently, on the mouth, the forehead, the cheeks.

"I'm glad I got to know you, Callie."

"Don't go," she said involuntarily. Her eyes were swimming in tears as she tried to see him clearly, wanting to imprint his image on her mind forever.

"I have to. Who knows, in a few months or a year, I might be back. And we can see what we have."

"I know what I have. You're the one who doesn't believe me," she whispered.

"Ah, honey, don't."

He pulled her against his chest, rubbing his hand over her back, cradling her head against his chest. "I remind you of Tommy. I've always known that."

"You're stupid like he was if that's what you believe. You don't remind me a bit of Tommy," she said, muffled against him. She could stay here forever.

"All my life I've battled to be my own person," he said. "Tommy loved playing up the twin feature, I wanted to downplay it."

She pulled back enough to see him.

"He's gone, Trace. I'm sorry for his death. He wasn't the man for me, but he didn't deserve to die so young. However, I don't see him when I look at you. You're strong and honorable and successful. You don't blame others for your actions or depend on others to exist. You love your parents even when they don't deserve it. You're dependable and compassionate. You know what's right and do it, no matter what the personal cost. I love you. I'll never forgive myself for the word murmured when I wasn't thinking, but I never once in all the time I've known you confused you with your brother. He's the unfinished version. You're complete. Go off to South America. Build your bridge. But when you're done, come back here and see me. See if you can find the love in you that burns so brightly in me. I want you. I want the home and kids and dogs and love that you and I together could have."

"You tempt a man. Maybe in a year or two. When you've forgotten him."

She pushed back and glared at him.

"Well, you tell yourself that, pigheaded man. I want you now. And I'm sure I'll want you in a year or two or ten. Is that what it'll take? Being faithful to only you for a decade before you'll believe what I say?"

"It's not that," he said.

"What then?"

"My mother had it wrong. Tommy and I didn't compete for the same girls in high school or college—what would be the point? I couldn't compare with his charming ways. If I was interested in a girl, he'd saunter over and before you knew it, she was falling beneath his spell. No competition."

"You never waited around long enough for them to fall out from beneath the spell, I bet. Then they see the dross instead of the gold. With you, it's all gold."

He pulled her closer and kissed her. "Hold that thought. I'll write."

He was gone before she could react.

She stared at the door for a long time, gradually realizing despite everything she'd said, he still didn't believe her.

Chapter Nineteen

Callie didn't move for the longest time, convinced he'd knock on the door, tell her he'd been an idiot and confess he loved her. The last few days had been heavenly. They had so much in common. Yet when they'd disagreed, they ended up laughing at the absurd lengths each would go to in order to make their point.

She could see them together in five years, ten, forty. Something she never saw with Tommy.

Finally she moved, dazed. He wasn't coming back.

She cleared the table, did the dishes, as if in a fog.

Lord, please help me to see the good in this. And if it's your will, let him come back.

When it was time for bed, she knew she wouldn't sleep. She grabbed her duvet and went out on her balcony. It was cool, the evening breeze damp from the sea. Wrapping up warmly, she sat in her chaise, gazing at the tiny sliver of lights reflected in the water blurred by the evening mist.

If she could relive one minute of her life and change it, it would be the one where she'd said Tommy's name when another man kissed her. One small thing which apparently was going to haunt her forever.

Trace drove back to the Inn, parked and got out. The evening mist gave everything a surreal look. He refused to let it dampen his mood.

He was too keyed-up to go to bed, so opted for a last walk through town. He'd gotten to know some of Rocky Point while he'd been here. It was a nice place. He'd like to come back in the off season and see what it was like then.

Callie would be here, unless she was on one of her buying trips.

Her words of love echoed in his mind. He wished he believed her. She was right, he didn't. Was he to battle the specter of his brother all his life? He was a grown man. Tommy was gone.

If he'd met Callie without her knowing Tommy, he'd never doubt her.

The sound of his brother's name on her lips when he kissed her echoed. Was he doomed to forever be second to his brother?

It was cool, but the damp air cleared his head. Gradually he began to think of the days ahead. He had the work at the bridge site to keep him busy. If she wrote, he'd write back. Maybe as he said, when he came back to the States, he'd come to see her again.

He wanted to turn around right now and storm back to her flat and tell her—tell her what? That he loved her even if she loved his brother?

All thoughts led back to Callie.

Finally growing tired, Trace returned to the Inn.

Her words of love echoed in his mind. The first time

anyone had put him ahead of Tommy. Was it only because Tommy was no longer around?

For the first time in his life, Trace listened to the words and believed them. He'd made a success of his life. He wasn't dependent on his parents, didn't flit from woman to woman without a thought of responsibility or duty. He didn't manipulate people.

And Callie said she loved him.

Dare he believe that?

The woman had a sterling reputation in town for being honest as the day was long. He'd heard plenty of comments the night of the opening.

He knew Callie would make him happy. Could he make her happy?

"I work in South America, in case you hadn't noticed," he argued with himself.

Could he trust Callie? That's what it all came down to

The pounding on the door woke her. It was still dark outside. Callie rose groggily and went to see if there was an emergency. What time was it? It felt like the middle of the night.

Throwing open the door she was stunned to see Trace standing there.

"What's wrong?" she asked. Had something happened to his parents?

He stepped inside and kissed her.

"My car's downstairs, I'm on my way to the airport. But I didn't sleep at all last night. I can't leave for Brazil without telling you I love you. I want you, too. Let's get married. As soon as I get back. I'll take what I can get and spend the next fifty years or so making you the husband you want."

"Wait a minute. Is this a proposal? You'll take what you can get?" she asked, heart pounding. It was what she wanted, just not the way she wanted it.

"I want you."

"Repeat after me, I believe you, Callie. You love me best."

He smiled. "I believe you, Callie, you love me best, and it had better stay that way forever!"

With a whoop of joy, Callie encircled his neck and pulled his face down for a kiss.

"Is that a yes?" Trace asked a minute later.

"Yes, of course it's a yes. I love you!"

"I love you. Marry me as soon as I get back from this assignment?"

"Yes. Wait, how long is that going to be?" She'd marry him tonight this morning, whatever time it was.

"Another eight or nine months, enough time to get everything lined up."

"And for you to miss most of the wedding planning."

"We'll be linked electronically—sporadically. Say yes, sweetheart, I have to catch that plane."

She hugged him tightly. "Don't go."

"I have to, but I'll be back, and then we'll find that house together and start on our family."

"What about bridges?"

"Don't they need them in America?"

"I guess."

"I can build other things, as well. Don't worry, you won't starve."

"Silly, I'm not worried about that. I want you doing what you want and what you're good at."

"I will. And we'll find a way to mesh our lives so I'm not out of the country while you're having our babies. I love you. Take a chance on me."

"I love you, Trace. There's no chance to take, only a blissful future."

He kissed her again.

"What changed your mind?" she asked breathlessly a few moments later.

"Tommy."

"What?"

"He died. What if I died and never knew what being married to you could be like? What if you died before I could tell you I loved you? Life's too uncertain to let things stall. I love you and am willing to put it right out there for all the world to know," he said.

"I plan to live to a hundred, just so you know," she said, hugging him tightly.

"Those match my own plans. Wait for me. I'll be back as soon as I get the bridge built."

"I'd wait until the end of time, Trace. I love you!"

The kiss he gave her had to last a long time. It almost did!

Epilogue

"Are you ready?" Trace asked, coming into the bedroom.

"Almost. What time is it?"

"Just after six."

"Yikes, we'll be late."

"They won't start without you."

"I can't be late on the opening night of the new gallery. I have a reputation to build in this town," she said primly.

"Ride on your reputation from Rocky Point," he said, leaning against the doorjamb and watching his wife of six months put the finishing touches on her makeup. He'd never tire of watching her. She was beautiful. He wanted to kiss that lipstick off and take her to bed.

But this was her big night and he was celebrating with her.

"Boston's an entirely different venue. No one here cares about Rocky Point," she said.

"Too bad, I like the place."

"Which is why we bought that house there. But Boston's

home now."

"Except for weekends when we head for Maine. Suzanne's the perfect manager."

"She was thrilled, wasn't she? I'm glad Marcie's catering this event tonight. I don't want anything to go wrong."

"Nothing will. My parents checked in earlier today. I talked to my father."

"I can't believe their support–your mother and your father using my new gallery exclusively. Along with recommendations to several of their colleagues. With that kind of backing, how can it fail?"

"It can't, but that's because of you, sweetheart, not the artwork you acquire."

She set down her brush, examined herself one last time then turned and walked to Trace. Reaching up, she kissed him.

"You're okay with working here in Boston?" she asked.

He'd received a new construction project, a high-rise office building near the downtown area.

"Yes."

She asked him that almost daily. He'd known what he was doing when he accepted the project. The months at the bridge site after proposing had seemed endless, even with the two or three e-mails a day from Callie–when they came through.

They'd grown to know each other well through their correspondence, but nothing beat being with her. He'd change careers before taking off again for months without her.

"Are you okay with living here instead of by the sea?" he asked.

"Boston's by the sea. I'll go to the docks anytime I need a salt water fix. I'm building an empire, you know. With the main gallery in Rocky Point, the second gallery that caters to tourists and now this one, I'll be a mogul in no time."

"If anyone deserves it, it's you. Don't stop. Why not a place in New York, as well."

She laughed. "Now you're dreaming. Let's get to the gallery. I have some news to share with you later."

"And that is?"

"Later, I said. You're all right with your parents staying at the hotel? We could have had them here," she said.

"Dad and I get along fine. But to Mom I'll always be second to Tommy. This is easier for both of us."

Callie reached out to touch his arm.

"You'll always be first to me," she said.

"It was nice of her to give us that painting she did after Tommy died for a wedding present--with the caveat you sell it," he said. "Any nibbles?"

"It's the centerpiece of tonight's exhibit. I've priced it exorbitantly. If it sells, it'll be a miracle. But it is wonderful. Just having it in my gallery will give us the cachet we need to be taken seriously."

"Not to mention Dad's sculptures."

"Wasn't that a coup? Wonder why he did that–switched to me exclusively, I mean."

"To keep it all in the family. Which reminds me, be prepared to be bored with a million pictures of little Tommy.

Mother carries around a ton of them on her phone and is always showing anyone who will stop long enough to look."

"Grandmothers should dote on their grandchildren. I'm just glad Teresa lets him visit them."

Trace kept quiet about the deal he'd made with the woman. As long as she allowed little Tommy to visit his grandparents, Trace supplemented the trust fund. Even though most of Tommy's paintings and a good portion of the pen-and-ink drawings had sold, so far the entire estate had not amounted to a great deal, divided as his will stated.

Trace's share had gone to little Tommy's trust. And he suspected his mother and father slipped the woman some money. He was fine with that. The little boy looked a lot like Tommy. Nothing would bring his brother back. But Trace liked seeing his brother in his son.

Callie looked up at him with mischief in her eyes. "I was going to wait, but I don't want to. We want equal time. Jocelyn and Montgomery will soon be grandparents a second time. I'm hoping for a girl, what about you?"

Trace looked at her, surprise and delight sweeping through him. "We're pregnant?"

"Due in seven months!"

He swept her up and spun her around. "Married six months and now we're going to be parents. Amazing!"

She smiled at his happiness. Trace knew then he'd made the right decision that night. Some risks were meant to be taken. Every day he knew he came first with Callie. And every day he gave thanks for the gift of her love.

"Guess you know what this means," she said.

"What?"

A new place to live–a house with a yard. Telling his parents. Telling hers. Would they wait for the Christmas visit?

"We need to decide the issue of art lessons. Personally I'm against them," she said, teasing. "I want us to be a happy family with no favorites and no stress about following in footsteps. Each child goes his or her own way."

"Deal!"

She laughed at his agreement, knowing he was happy.

She gave thanks every day for his coming into her life. Only when reminded by Jocelyn or Montgomery did she give any thought to the young man she'd once been engaged to. He was so far removed from her husband she never understood how she could have been fooled into thinking she loved him.

When the real thing appeared, she knew the other had been nothing, a girl's first venture into infatuation.

"I love you, Callie," Trace said softly.

"I love you, Trace, always and forever."

Her vow was sealed with another kiss.

—The End—

Did you enjoy this story? If so you may enjoy
Rocky Point Box Set Books 1-3 or **Mail Order Bride**

More books by Barbara McMahon

The Harts of Texas Series
Rebel Heart
Tangled Hearts
Reckless Heart

Cowboy Heroes Series
Blue Bells on the Hill
Cowboy's Bride
One Stubborn Cowboy
Crazy About a Cowboy
Never Doubt a Cowboy
Cowboy Marshal
Summer Cowboy
Second Chance Cowboy
Movie Star Cowboy

Tropical Escape Series
Island Rendezvous
Come into the Sun
Island Paradise
Destination Romance Boxed Set

Elite Security Mystery Series
Trusting Jake

Rocky Point Series
Rocky Point Legacy
Rocky Point Reunion
Rocky Point Promise
Rocky Point Hero
Rocky Point Inn

The Ultimate Billionaires
The Cynical Sheikh
Falling for the Sheikh
A Sheikh of Her Own
The Unforgettable Sheikh

Other Books
A Soldier's Christmas
I'll Take Forever
Jared's Promise
The Paper Marriage
The Christmas Locket
The Banished Bride
Cowboy Charade
The Cowboy's Special Christmas
Mail Order Bride
Because of You
Sweet Meant To Be

www.ingramcontent.com/pod-product-compliance
Lightning Source LLC
Chambersburg PA
CBHW071307250626
47159CB00004B/1341